Revenge of the Marquis Cartel

James Marquis

REVENGE OF THE MARQUIS CARTEL

James Marquis

FOREWORD

This book is the last of the trilogy, which covers love, passion, death, violence, destruction, and the creation of the largest cartel in the CaribbeanSea, The Marquis Cartel. It was able to exist due to the support of two major crime organizations being that of the Black Disciples and King's Jamaican Cutthroats. Ron, Jim, David were known as the powerbrokers of the Marquis Cartel. They were targeted for assassination by El Capo and his Cartel. Jim's loss of his second lover, Ron, puts him in a downward spiral leading him to emotional ruin along with his imprisonment. His life has never changed this dramatically. The once highly respected Marquis Cartelnow sits paralyzed, waiting for its leaders to reappear.

CONTENTS

THE PENAL INSTITUTION

*A*s his prison van approached the Pennsylvania penitentiary, Jim thoughtback to Ron crying out for help on the Tito IV after he was shot. He remembered how he stood shell-shocked in the hospital's emergency room. As he was being told of his lover's death, the FBI handcuffed him and hauled him off to that decrepit jail in Costa Rica. Those thoughts are now nightmares that he will have to endure for years to come. As the van arrives at the prison, he and the other inmates are lined up in the receiving room to be strip-searched.

Being strip-searched was honestly not frightening for Jim, for he was used to displaying his manhood boldly around even the grisliest of killers. He was one of twenty in line and was so pretty that other inmates immediately took notice. It was quite obvious to even the jailers that he was a thoroughbred from the wealthy side of the track. He was so well-groomed and polished that his appearance alone should be a major concern for him in the years to come.

Jim began to hear whispers sputter about amongst the inmates, and suddenly a barely audible mutter came across his ears saying, "he will be eaten alive in here!" Jim knew this was about him. Hethought that he had to reduce that big target on his head or, at a bare minimum, become a commodity himself so he could survive in this haggard bastille.

With the in-processing ordeal now complete, he was assigned to his first jail cell on the penitentiary's second floor. They assigned cellmates by gang affiliation, race, and religion to help diminish the possibilities of fights and slayings. Jim was led by the guard to this 6x10 dilapidated cell that was an even tighter squeeze than the hooch he shared in Vietnam. When entering his new dwellings, he saw a large figure tucked in the corner of thebottom bunk.

The darkened figure grumbled, "Now, who are you?"

With a slight bit of hesitation, Jim answered, "Jim… Your new bunkmate." The darkened figure then replied, "What are you in here for?"

Again Jim answered with a bit of hesitation and said, "Money laundering and assault on a federal agent.

"You must be all kinds of stupid," said the darkened figureas he began to slowly roll over, revealing himself. There he stood, all 5'7" and 260 pounds of all gut. His knotted brown hair fell lazily down to his shoulders, his goatee long and unkept helped distract from the acne dotting his face thickened with grease. He introduced himselfas Jonah and told Jim what he was imprisoned for before anyone else could and for good reasons. Jonah was convicted of rape when he was eighteen years old and is serving a twenty-five-year sentence. In prison, rapists tend to have a target automatically placed on their back as soon as they walk through the door and are among the lowest rungs of the ladder.

Jim had no knowledge of the prison system's hierarchy, but he alreadycould tell this man was not worth his shit. He had been imprisoned for five years and was nothing special to look at. Jim thought, *No wonderhe had to rape a girl, for no girl would have him.*

When Jim settled in, Jonah established the cell rules, which were: stay out of my way, and I'll stay out of yours.

Jim said, "It will be kind of hard to do so in these small quarters."

Jonah replied, "When I'm up and about, stay on your top bunk."

Jim didn't acknowledge the conversation. He was thoroughly disgusted with Jonah and was livid that he was at first frightened of this fat, pock-marked barrel of lard. Jim took a deep breath and sighed to himself. He would have to get along with this pig in order to make his stay even a little bit more bearable.

Part of Jim's sentence dictated that he was to have no public contact during his first year either in person or via the mail with any individual outside of the prison. He was effectively dead to the world. That meant that he had no one to deposit funds in his prison account, which was used for commissary items and phone calls. The only way he would get the items he needed was through the bartering system, and all he had to barter with was his body. He damn well knew how to do that. During his first prison yard experience, he cruised the compound, looking for likely candidates to pair up with. One of the few rules he did pick up in prison was that there were no homosexual activities allowed on the premises. However, he also knew that sex still happened behind closed doors. As he cruised the yard, he made note of the several guys that had their eyes on him.

Later that night in the room, Jonah said, "You're a halfway good-looking dude; I noticed that several guys in the yard had their eye on you. What are you into?"

Jim didn't reply or acknowledge that he heard the question. Jonah stripped down to his boxers and started to vigorously stroke his small stubby nub while he was leaning against the sink so that Jim could watch the "magic." Again, Jim didn't respond or acknowledge the event. Jonah began to become more desperate for Jim's attention. He was extremely horny and reached down to Jim's bunk and tapped Jim on his shoulder, asking him if he would like to assist him. Jim gave him a burning death stare and, with a deep biting voice, told him to get his fucking hands off him. Jim would rather choke to death on his own vomit rather than be involved with that greasy corpulent slob.

A few days passed, and Jim started to feel in need, not for sex but for soap, shampoo, toothpaste, proper underwear to enhance his manhood, and funds for his commissary account. A series of fortunate events lead a man named Heath to corner Jim in the shower and ask him if he wanted to have a little fun. Heath wasn't bad looking; Jim thought he somewhat reminded Jim of King from Jamaica.

Jim came right out and told Heath, "I need some commissary items first, then I'll give it to you." Heath replied, "How much?"

Jim replied, "Transfer fifty dollars to me, and when

it hits my account, I will meet you back here and give you all that you can handle and more."

Heath was more than agreeable. Two days later, they met in the shower room, and Heath got his manhole penetrated with sheer delight. Heath had no idea that Jim was going to take charge as dominantly as he had done. He was even more amazed by the size of Jim's member, which evidently was a grower, not a shower. Jim was both rough and passionate with Heath, slamming him against the shower wall and pressing his head against the cold, wet tile as he dominated him completely. The moment was so intense that Heath could barely subdue his screams of pleasure while Jim performed his commissary deposit ritual.

After Jim's performance with Heath, it became widely known throughout the prison that Jim would barter sexual acts for commissary deposits to his account. By the end of six weeks, Jim had more than $1,000 in his commissary account and a raw manhole. For Jim to bottom, it would cost a hundred dollars deposit. Jim took precautions against HIV. He required all his tricks to provide or use condoms smuggled into the prison through various means. As weeks slowly turned into months, there were even more guys Jim had to choose from, building up his clientele base.

He carefully ventured into the Puerto Rican and Mexican prisoners' territory. When he crossed over into that prison side, things changed for the worse. They didn't pay or barter for sex. They just took it, and Jim was now on their radar. It was common knowledge throughout the prison that Jim was essentially an easy mark and would perform any sexual act necessary. Unbeknownst to Jim was that he soon would be in for the fight for his life due to this fact.

One day in the yard, when he decided to join a group of Puerto Ricans for a smoke, he was approached by a rather rugged Puerto Rican, 5'7", 160 lbs. with a mustache named Blade.

He said, "I hear you're a good fuck," in a thick Spanish account. "How many of those white boys have you fucked since you got here?"

Jim just looked at him with his menacing death stare and proceeded to walk on. Blade took that reaction as rejection, and he did not tolerate being rejected. Blade smiled and informed Jim that he would be seeing him later. Jim carried on with that response in his mind wondering what the results would be.

A couple of days passed, and Jim proceeded to the shower as he normally did, but as he walked into the shower room, something was different. His usual shower mates were not there; in fact, the entire shower was empty. Seeing his shower mates was one of the few bright spots he still had in his life, and on occasion, enjoying those naked bodies helped keep his spirits up. When he was halfway through his shower, he felt a strong hand around his mouth and another around his waist, which jerked him into the wall.

A voice in his ear said, "My name is Buck. And it's time to fuck!" Then out came a big boisterous "Woooo" as a hand grabbed Jim's ass with enough strength to crush a can. The man engulfing Jim's body with his own suddenly leaned over as if he was looking behind him. Out of the corner of Jim's eye, he saw Blade walking into the shower with another two men. He knew instantly what was going to go down. Blade walked up in front of them, and the guy holding him forced Jim to kneel as Blade grabbed Jim roughly by the hair and savagely stuck his cock in Jim's mouth and told him to suck it as he slapped him across the face.

"No teeth," Blade demanded as he roughly shoved his cock even deeper. Jim proceeded as instructed. Blade's cock was so thick and long that Jim could not swallow it. Not satisfied, Blade moved to Jim's other hole. He soon realized that if Blade were going to fuck him with that monster of a cock, he would obliterate his manhole. Blade gave no care at all to Jim's pain or pleasure and violently destroyed his manhole without mercy. Jim felt like it took a lifetime for Blade to satisfy himself only to switch positions with the other guys who were holding him down, who pleasured themselves as well.

Within about an hour or more, Jim had been fucked by four Puerto Ricans who left Jim lying on the shower room floor, beaten and bleeding from his rectum and crying in pain. This is the first time Jim had ever been treated like a worthless whore in his entire life; it was amongst one of the worst experiences in his life. Something he would never forget or fully heal from. When he got back to his cell, he went directly to bed and had nightmares all night long of his brutal rape.

When he woke in the morning, there was blood on his sheets from his ass that was still so sore that he could barely walk. He crawled out of bed and went to the sink, got a washcloth, and cleaned his ass as best he could while tearing up from the pain. He slowly began dressing afterward for breakfast. Every movement he made sent an excruciating pain rippling through him. As Jim stumbled down the hallway for chow, it seemed like everyone was looking at him and knew that he had just been raped by the Puerto Ricans. He attempted to elude all direct eye contact, ate as fast as he could, and returned to his cell. As soon as Jonah walked in, Jim said he needed a favor from him. Jonah was taken completely by surprise as Jim had not talked directly to him with any type of sincerity in his voice before then.

Jonah asked as to what he needed, for he must be desperate asking him for anything.

Jim said, "Do you have any friends in this facility?"

"What kind of friends?"

"Tough gang friends."

"Why do you want to know?"

Jim said in almost a whisper, "I was raped by the Puerto Ricans, and I'm afraid for my life."

Jonah sat on the bunk next to him with a look of disbelief on his face. "Well, Jim, you been bartering sex for commissary funds since you got here. It was about time that someone showed you how inmates treat faggots. You have been flaunting it for the last year, and it was more than time for you to pay what you owe. You didn't even so much as let me get a piece of it, and you want a favor from me! Why don't you prove to me that you really need this favor?"

With no other option, Jim put a rag over the window at the door and crawled in the bunk next to

Jonah. He started to caress his fat body, and Jonah's stubby fat cock stood erect. When Jim got that far, he saw that all of Jonah's pubic hair was shaved off, which was a complete turnoff to him, and his balls were sucked deep into his fat body and didn't show. Jim had never been so turned off while attempting to have some type of sexual activity with an individual as he did at this very moment. Jim's stomach turned at the thought of having to put that rough sweaty dick in his mouth. He thought to himself he would rather get fucked by it, despite the pain of last night, than to attempt to swallow that ugly rough dick.

He asked Jonah, "How you want it?"

Jonah flipped him over and proceeded without a thought given of Jim's previous rape. Jonah was quick to reach a climax as he had not been pleasured for multiple years. After they were finished, Jim rushed to the sink to clean his bleeding manhole before returning to his upper bunk.

After about an hour, Jonah said, "Come down here. I want to talk to you." He said, "If you please me on a more regular basis, I'll connect you with a few people that I know that could protect you. But they have a price as well. Nothing is free in this place, not even friendship."

Jim remembered the shower experience with the Puerto Ricans, which he did not want to repeat. He told Jonah that he would like to consider his offer. Jonah was quick to establish a routine for when he was to be pleasured, and Jim agreed to that. Jonah said that after their part of the deal was fulfilled for a while, the introduction would be made. Jim thought, *how long will I have to endure this humiliation to secure my safety?*

Jonah started his nightly rituals of being satisfied orally and anally while at the same time more Puerto Ricans began to harass and demand sex from Jim. This lasted for a couple of days until Jonah was satisfied that Jim was keeping up his end of the bargain. At the end of this period, Jim was just disgusted with himself that he had to be so humiliated by such a fat beast to get the protection he needed. Jonah then told Jim that he would set up a meeting with his contacts tomorrow.

PRESERVATION

The next day in the yard, Jonah and Jim were surrounded by fifteen of the most tattooed white guys in the prison. They chatted with Jonah while Jim was smoking a cigarette at the end of the bleachers while he was watching the Puerto Ricans playing basketball. He knew full well that they were talking about him and trying to establish some type of game plan to satisfy everyone's needs. One of the tattooed guys named Logan approached Jim. He was a tough-looking motherfucker, someone you did not want to piss off at all.

"Jim, I hear you got a problem that you need help with."

"Affirmative."

"So, you need our help, but you know it doesn't come cheap, right?"

"Just tell me how you want to be paid and how much."

Logan sat down next to him on the bleachers putting his large, heavy arm around his shoulders, and said, "The word around the yard is that you have a bartering system, and you now know how it works in here. You've cashed in your ass for a pretty dollar. And what a pretty ass you got."

Jim replied, "We all have to survive here; I did what I had to do."

Logan looked at him and said, "You're right; we all have to survive here. Do you want to survive, Jim?"

"I do, or I wouldn't be here. So, what do I need to do, Logan?"

"There's fifteen of us," Logan said. "We all need satisfaction to some degree. Taking on the Puerto Ricans is not a simple task; they are a rough bunch. We'll have to plan out everything to protect you. When can you visit me in my cell?"

Jim looked him over while contemplating his decision. Logan was about 6' tall with blonde hair and a full beard. He was about 225 pounds of pure muscle and had a well-chiseled six-pack with blonde hair covering his chest. Jim's mind started to race, and he had to snap out of it.

"Tonight, at what time?" Jim said.

Logan said, "After chow, that gives us a few hours before lights are out.

Jim had dinner with Jonah that night which was not his usual routine. He was curious and asked about Logan.

Jonah smirked and said, "You'll find out. You can tell me all about it when you get back to our cell tonight."

Jim started to count down the minutes until he had to report to Logan's cell. At exactly 6:15 pm, Jim knocked on Logan's door. When he opened it, he was surprised to see Logan standing shirtless alongside his cellmate.

"Come on in."

Jim walked in, and Logan put a rag over the window and said, "Sit there on the bed and let's have a little talk."

Logan introduced him to his cellmate. Raymond stood 6'1" with black curly hair all over his body. His closely shaven beard and dark brown eyes captivated Jim when he shook his hand. Jim was surprised how soft his hands were and the sheer length of his fingers that seemed to wrap all around his hand, giving it a firm squeeze.

Jim said, "It's a pleasure to meet you." Both of them sat across from Jim. Logan pulled his chair up close to Jim while Raymond sat on the counter next to the sink.

Raymond began the conversation by saying, "We understand you need our help."

Jim looked Raymond directly in the eyes and said, "Yes, yes, I do."

At this point, Jim was wondering who was exactly in charge. Was it Logan with his bold, masculine appearance or Raymond with the sexy soft persona of a man who could dominate you with his looks alone? Jim was utterly confused. He then remembered the dynamics of his relationship with King and how they were an odd pairing that worked so well.

Raymond said, "You know you let the worst possible group get the best of you. The Puerto Ricans are as tough as they are ruthless. We only deal with them when we have to. We've lost a few of our own in brawls with them over the years. You flaunted your ass around this prison for a whole year advertising it without any consideration for your safety. You only thought about how easy the money was and getting what you wanted as usual pretty boy.

"Well, that was a fucking stupid idea. Anyone can tell you that you've never been to prison before. And everybody could tell that you are the prissy type who is divorced from the notion of what manual labor is. So, tell me something I don't already know about you from just looking at you," Raymond demanded.

Jim felt it was time to be open and honest because his life depended on it. He went on to talk about his life before he was arrested for money laundering and assaulting that prick of a federal agent. His deceased lover, the leader of the notorious Jamaican gang, the Cutthroats, and he, were all leaders of the Marquis Cartel, controlling all of the Caribbean Sea drug movement.

"While in Panama, we were attacked by a Guatemalan Cartel headed by a man named "Little El Capo" when we were trying to leave the docks. My lover was wounded in the shootout and died at the hospital that day. While still at the hospital, I was apprehended by the FBI for money laundering before I could even wipe a tear from my face. I then was held in a crappy Panamanian jail till I was extradited to the United States, tried, and convicted. I was sentenced to ten years and was recommended here by that prick of an agent. That's the short story. What more would you like to know?"

Raymond and Logan looked at each other, a bit dumbfounded.

Logan then asked Jim if he still had any connections in Jamaica.

"Yes. I have my entire network based out of Jamaica; why do you ask?"

"You have put us in a very delicate position. Logan and I lead the white contingency here in the prison. They don't question our decisions or what we do. They follow our orders, and they do what we tell them. End of story. We have been here together for seven years now. We were transferred here together after serving several years in different prisons, and we later arranged to live together. I will not go into the details, but just know that we have people.

"We were convicted of human trafficking by various islands in the Caribbean Sea. We had our rules by which we did not handle underage women or men under any circumstances. The transports in question were all prearranged via their own correspondents who made all the connections with us happen. Our operation is still in existence till this day and is based out of the Dominican Republic. So, if you can provide us some assistance with our operation, we will provide you with security here in prison. It's as simple as that, but of course, we are open to some casual side benefits too."

Jim looked at the two of them and slowly asked, "Are you two a couple?"

Logan replied quickly and earnestly, "Yes, I'm telling you this in complete confidence. Do you understand me? You repeat that to anyone, and you will find yourself dead before the words can fully leave your lips. Logan and I have been together for fifteen years. We have been able to survive in prison due to our ruthless leadership, and the fact that we are a couple means that you will never divide our power. You can only draw double our wrath."

"Consider your request done if you have a way of communicating to Jamaica," Jim said.

"We have phone privileges that you don't have," Raymond replied.

Logan interjected, "Before we get to all of the details of that, you can... no, you—will share with us tonight. We want to see what all these Puerto Ricans are going crazy for."

Jim knew exactly what they wanted and had no hesitation in showing them what made all the boys go crazy. He stripped down to his birthday suit and stood before them in all his manly glory and said, "Let me see what you both got."

Logan and Raymond looked at each other and smiled, then they followed suit. Jim's eyes examined every inch of their beautiful bodies right down to their toes. It had been a long time since he had seen such raw masculinity. Logan with all of his lush blonde hair and Raymond with those thick black curly locks draping his body as if it was a cape. Jim's mouth began to water just looking at the two. He didn't know how they wanted to start.

Jim laid back on the lower bunk and said, "Is this where you want me?"

Raymond said, "That will do for starters." He crawled in on top of Jim and smothered him with that thick black hair, and Jim spread his legs and felt Raymond's manhood enter him. Jim felt no pain, nothing but sheer pleasure as Raymond ravished him over and over again, smothering him as Raymond came to a climax inside of him.

Raymond then got up exhausted and said, "God, that was good, Jim. Come on, Logan, get some of this exquisite ass."

Logan said, "I can't without you, Raymond, so join me."

Logan flipped Jim on his side with his face against the wall, entering his manhole from behind as Raymond took advantage of Logan's body. His tongue ravished him from his ankles to his neck and then penetrated him with his manhood from behind. Jim's body shivered with pure delight with Logan inside him, for

Logan drove home his immense piece of manhood that Jim could not help but enjoy. The indescribable sexual event ended when all three climaxed simultaneously, and they collapsed on the bottom bunk together.

Two days later, Logan placed a call to Jamaica and handed the phone to Jim. He had the operator in Jamaica dial King's number at his townhouse. The number was forwarded to a new number that Jim did not recognize, but King picked up the phone. He was so happy to hear Jim's voice and couldn't stop telling him how much he missed him and was waiting for him to get home. Jim told King that he needed a favor, explained the situation, and then put Logan on the phone. Logan talked to King briefly, giving him detailed instructions on how to contact his organization in the Dominican Republic. King said it will be taken care of and for Logan to call back within four days and he would have a reply. Logan and King hung up the phone.

He, Jim, and Raymond joined Jonah in the yard. When they were all in the yard, the entire group surrounded them so that others could not tell who or what they were discussing. It was obvious to the Puerto Ricans that Logan's group was now protecting Jim. However, there was still one guy in the Puerto Rican group still interested in Jim; his name was Jerome.

Jerome had heard rumors from around the yard that Jim was the leader of a Cartel and affiliated with the notorious Panamanian gang, The Black Disciples. One way or another, Jerome wanted to make contact with Jim to let him know that he, too, was a member of the Black Disciple gang in Panama. So, Jerome began to time Logan and Raymond's showering schedule, for he knew the only way he would be able to get to Jim was to go through either of them first.

One night when Logan and Raymond took a late shower, Jerome cautiously entered the shower exposing his beautiful Puerto Rican body. He glanced over at Raymond and nodded with a smile on his face to not pose as a threat. Surprisingly, Raymond nodded back. Jerome had set in motion the first nonverbal communication necessary to establish a relationship with the white gang's leaders. He joined them in the shower for several days. Each day he continued his nonverbal communication and stood closer to them in the shower. On several occasions, he got an erection of great length, allowing them to know that he was comfortable and displayed vulnerability.

It took about two weeks, and Raymond was the one who spoke up first, "Can I help you with something, friend?"

Jerome said, "Yes, I want to know if we can be friends? I may be Puerto Rican, but I have the same gang affiliation with the man under your protection, Jim. I want him to know that I'm a Black Disciple member too."

Raymond said, "I realize that you have much to lose by appearing to us or around us. But as you should know, nothing in life is free, not even conversation."

"I am well aware of that."

Raymond replied, "Then what are you going to offer us to relay this message that you consider so important that you are willing to risk your livelihood and standing for?"

Under Jerome's towel was a bag containing 10 packs of cigarettes and a bottle of pruno (Jailhouse wine). He handed the bag to Raymond and said, "I will transfer commissary items to you every day this week. I'll need a secure way of giving you these items without being found out. So how do you suggest we arrange a meeting?"

Raymond said, "Let me think about that."

When Jim met with Raymond and Logan, they told him that they had met a member of the Black Disciples in the shower room. Raymond asked, "How do we know if we can trust him? For all we know, this could be a clever ploy by the Puerto Ricans to lure you out of our safety and make an example of you."

Jim said, "The leader of the Black Disciples is Leroy, and his two brothers are named Lloyd and Devon. If he gives you their names, have him describe them and their habits in detail and get back to me. I know enough about them, and if his description is correct, I know he can be trusted. Raymond said that they usually meet Jerome in the shower every night, so they will question him when he shows up again."

The next night Jerome showed up when Raymond and Logan were having their usual shower. Raymond immediately asked Jerome the Black Disciples' leaders' names and to describe them in detail and any of their defining habits.

Immediately Jerome rattled off, "Leroy, Lloyd, and Devon. Leroy is the gang leader, and all three brothers are gay. It's not a secret throughout the higher part of the organization that they are all gay, but it is not discussed casually, for you would be marked for death. Devon is bisexual, Leroy is a top, and Lloyd's a power bottom. I've known them for quite a while and had the pleasure of engaging in some of their sexual escapades. They're particularly good friends of mine and are the sole reason why I receive what money and protection that I get here. If you mention my name to them, they will say they know me."

When Raymond and Logan met with Jim the following day, they told him what Jerome had said. Jim said that it matched 100% with the description of the three leaders of the Black Disciples. He then asked if Jerome could be transferred in with him.

Logan took charge this time and said, "I'll check with my connections to see if that's possible. But Jerome would be putting his life at risk by integrating with a white person under our protection. We would have to think up a real valid excuse for his transfer so as not to raise suspicion. Let's think about it."

About a week passed, and when Jim met with Logan and Raymond, Logan spoke up. He said that they were able to get Jerome transferred in with Jim under the following condition: Jerome will have to state that he had been sexually threatened by a Puerto Rican gang member and fears for his life. He would feel more protected transferring in with a white gang member for protection, but not so much in those words.

"We can arrange for him to be bunked with you. When we see Jerome in the shower tonight, we'll run this idea past him to see if he's comfortable with it."

Jerome was originally hesitant about the idea but agreed to it. The only issue was finding a fall guy that would solidify their plan. After some thought and convincing, he chose a friend to act as if he had assaulted him and compensated him for his discretion. After that, the transfer was completed that week. So now Jim and Jerome were not only bunkmates, but they also shared the same connections with the Black Disciples.

Jim never thought in a million years that he would find anyone who may know of him or even know some of the same people he knew. This was more than a welcome surprise to him and put him at ease, for he could finally talk to someone that he can relate to on multiple levels. Jerome introduced himself to Jim and began where most prisoners start, with what they are incarcerated for. He said that he was convicted of attempted murder and armed robbery and was serving a ten-year sentence. He was now in the seventh year of his sentence and could be paroled at any time.

Jerome and Jim's relationship immediately began to bloom quite beautifully. Jerome was handsome. Being of Puerto Rican and Venezuelan ancestry, he had a smooth Spanish accent with short curly hair.

He had a special sparkle in his appearance that simply turned Jim on. In the beginning, Jim didn't let on that he was sexually attracted to Jerome because he did not want to complicate their friendship. Finally,

Jerome broke the ice. Late one night, he covered the window to their prison door, went down to Jim's lower bunk, crawled into his bed, and deepthroated Jim while grabbing his ass. He ravished his blonde hair from his armpits to his toes. Jim exploded in Jerome's mouth, and he almost gagged with the amount of Jim juice that he had to swallow quickly to make room for more. They both agreed that was a wonderful experience for both of them. That night was the beginning of their monogamous relationship for the rest of Jim's prison term.

Jerome told Jim that the Black Disciples made weekly deposits to his commissary account. He would never have to worry about going without funds. In the fifth year of his ten-year sentence, Jim had a similar arrangement where King made sure that his commissary account was loaded to the till. They had a nice small color television for entertainment and rarely associated with other prisoners except for Logan and Raymond occasionally.

During the years Jim was in prison, he corresponded with King and Leroy to formulate plans for when he was released from prison. King had absorbed Jim's remaining cartel into his organization and was running it quietly behind the scenes. The money that Ron had established in multiple bank accounts all over the world was still there. Jim was thankful that Ron had told him all of the bank accounts he had opened and where all the records were kept on the Tito IV. It had not been impounded by the U.S. due to it being registered to an LLC. The yacht was still being used by King with the original crew members, tucked deep into the Caribbean. Luckily for Jim, not too much changed in his time away. He would have access to all of this information upon his release from prison.

When Jim was convicted of money laundering and tax evasion, it was due to his using funds out of his secret bank account to buy the Tito IV and the island all within one week. The island's owner and the yacht broker both deposited the money in the same US bank. That set off the red flags for his arrest because the amount he spent far exceeded the amount he reported being worth. However, the Marquis Cartel accounts were never affected and remained loaded with money, ready for **REVENGE.**

A FRESH START

*J*im got an early release from prison for good behavior. The majority of his seven years were spent with Jerome. He was grateful to the Black Disciples and King for their financial support during his prison term. The day he was released from prison, he took a flight back to Jamaica and a taxi to the Royal Jamaican yacht club where the Tito IV was moored. The crew was standing at attention alongside the yacht in their white uniforms to welcome Jim back on board. The yacht looked as new as it was the day he left, and the crew had tears in their eyes from the joy of seeing him finally home.

After all of them gathered in the man cave having a few drinks and catching up on the goings-on in their lives, Jim placed a call to King and told him he had finally arrived home and to please come to dinner. Needless to say, King emphatically agreed and said that he would be there immediately. Once he arrived, King grabbed Jim and retreated to the master suite for several hours of prolonged sex that was far beyond the sloppy and dirty sex. It was a blend of both nightmares and dreams mixed into one long session of deep passion. After a long hot shower, they both reappeared on the back deck for drinks and dinner.

Chef Timothy prepared the latest of his outstanding dinners: filet mignon, lobster, baked sweet potato, sweet peas, and homemade apple pie for dessert. Due to Jim's prolonged absence, the crew had become like family on the yacht. They were no longer treated as hired help but recognized as members of the Marquis Cartel. During dinner, they started to strategize their comeback as the most powerful cartel in the Caribbean Sea. King's organization had quietly but successfully controlled the remainder of the loyal exporters. However, their income did diminish significantly to about $9,000,000 a month. This covered all of their expenses with a little reserve. This reserve was in cash on the island that they still owned.

The next morning, with King still on board, they set out for the island where members of King's organization were permanently housed. Simon and Adams were no longer employed as mercenaries as

King's organization replaced them. King's Cutthroats numbered in the hundreds and could be dispatched by fast boats anywhere in the Caribbean Sea. King had supervised constructing an enormous peer on the island so that the yacht could be moored and fast boats could be tied up more easily. He had built two mansions: one of substantial size, the other smaller in nature held members of his organization. The property had guard posts surrounding it and was guarded 24/7. The island had the most up-to-date electronic surveillance systems available and cameras spread around the island's coastline so it could be surveyed from remote sites within both structures on the island.

All the managers of the import-export offices from Venezuela to Panama and the Caribbean were transferred to King's organization. Alex from Panama and Jamison from Venezuela lived aboard the yacht, while Wayne from Grand Cayman's and Butch from Jamaica lived on the island. Alex was a favorite of most of the men who were either onboard or frequented the yacht. Still, whenever the Black Disciples came aboard, LeRoy made it known that Alex was his and his alone. Alex had this exotic allure about him, from the way he moved, the clothes he wore, and by the way he talked, and Leroy found it absolutely intoxicating. This bond between Alex and Leroy further cemented the bonds between the Black Disciples and the Marquis Cartel. It led to many nights of aggressive passion between the two. Neither could leave the night without some type of mark, whether it be a bite mark, scratches, or gentle bruises from spankings.

Now that the yacht crew are now part of the Marquis cartel and would be staying onboard as associates, Jim and King needed to hire a new crew to run the yacht. As in the past, Jim asked everyone to join him in the man cave for drinks to discuss replacements for their positions and if they had any referrals in mind. Jim asked Captain John if he had any thoughts about retiring. Captain John said that he could put in another five years as captain of the yacht, which he genuinely enjoyed.

Collectively the crew came up with recommendations for all of the positions that needed to be filled. The individuals they recommended were all gay and currently working on or have served on a yacht, so they all were qualified. They told Jim that he would have to run the security background check on the individuals and complete the nondisclosure agreements since they don't have Simon and Adam anymore.

There have been a lot of changes in everyone on the yacht. Here's a recap of who reside aboard the Tito IV:

Jim and King

Alex (former manager of the Panama operation)

Jamison (former manager of the Dominican Republic operation)

Butch – (former manager of the Jamaican operation)

Wayne – (former manager of the Grand Cayman operation)

Timothy (former chef)

Andrew (former steward)

Stephen (former deckhand)

Simon – Head of Security

The new crew onboard the Tito IV:

Captain John

Chef Jeff – full-time chef

Chief Steward Keith – supervises staterooms/laundry/service

Steward JP – state rooms/laundry/server

Steward/Deckhand Winston -state rooms/laundry/server/deckhand

Deckhand George – full-time deckhand

The Tito IV crew was increased by two due to the increased number of people living aboard. All of the individuals recommended passed their security checks, and all the necessary paperwork was completed. After the break-in period, the yacht and the new crew were operating at 100% efficiency. Jim and King were now in the midst of a detailed plan for the Marquis Cartel's future. An unusual postcard was received in the mail addressed to Jim from David, welcoming him back to the yacht, but the card did not show a return address, only a postmark from Madrid, Spain. Jim was desperate to get a hold of David. He would be essential in the intricate planning necessary to get revenge on El Capo's cartel.

DAVID

$\mathcal{T}$he postcard reflected Jim's need for David's analytical and technical skills as well as the love he held for him. David had always been the backbone of Jim and Ron's decision-making process. Not only did they trust him, but they loved him, and their platonic love was so strong that Jim yearned for him to be by his side now more than ever. During the past seven years, Jim had mourned Ron's death every day and every night. Similarly, he still mourned Tito's death over the years, and he soon concluded that whoever he loves is fated for death. He vowed to himself that he would never fall in love again and would harden his heart so he will never know the gentle touch of love anymore. His relationships from now on will be either platonic or sexual, but not a relationship of "love," for he could not take losing yet another person in his life.

He felt truly fortunate that Ron had taught him how to decipher the cartel books in detail. He understood where all the money was, how it flowed, how it was transferred, where to transfer it for safekeeping, and how to withdraw it a little at a time without detection. This time he will not get careless, especially since he now is the only one who can manage the cartel's funds properly. The staff payroll accounts were still at the same bank as before, and their automatic transfers were well-established. He dove into the books to find out where they had transferred the money to David so that he could trace his transactions. By tracing his transactions, he could see the towns in which David was residing. The last transaction was from Madrid, Spain, as was the postcard.

Jim called King and asked if he maintained any connections in Madrid that could be of assistance in locating David. King said that he would check things out and let Jim know. About two hours later, King called with the name and phone number of GYS Security Services, the same company used to employ Simon and Adam. It's a global operation with operatives all over the world. King said to contact them and see if they could help. Jim placed a phone call to GYS and inquired if they could assist in locating an individual in Madrid, Spain. They transferred the call to Jake Davenport, the same account officer that they had used before. He greeted Jim warmly and took down David's information, and told him that he would get back to him as soon as they had some news to report.

The next morning Jake phoned in with David's address and phone number in Madrid. He said that David was employed as a personal assistant to a very wealthy individual whose name he could not divulge due to procedure. David could be contacted at the telephone number that he provided. Jim told him to send the bill to the yacht's address and thanked him for such speedy results. Jim immediately placed a call to David, who answered on the second ring.

When he answered, Jim said, "Is this my long-lost lover?"

David said immediately without hesitating, "Jim! How did you find me?"

"How I found you doesn't matter; I need you, David. I want you to join me back on the yacht, you are an integral part of my life and plans, and nothing will get done without you. If you would have me again, fly back to Jamaica. I'll be at the Royal Jamaican Yacht Club, slip number one. That's where I will be waiting for you."

Before Jim could finish with what he had to say, David said, "Jim, I'll be on the next flight out."

David and Jim's reunion was a sight to behold. Over the seven years they had been separated, the years had been more difficult for David than Jim could ever imagine. Even though he had all the money in the world, he lacked the love necessary to enjoy life. Reunited, David felt that love that surrounded him when he was with Ron and Jim in the past. The Tito IV was always his home, and he now knew it. He settled into his old stateroom, took a long hot shower, introduced himself to the new crew members, and settled in with Jim in the man cave to have a few drinks. He sat there admiring Jim's handsome face that had dimmed from his memory over the years. Jim noticed almost instantly that David had changed from an immature, childlike person to an adult's hardened appearance. He asked David if life was hard on him during the last seven years, for he seemed more somewhat depressed as well.

"It's a cruel world out there without love. When the three of us were together, even when the bullets were flying, I was happy because I knew I was loved. And that love kept me safe, Jim. You always protected me, and living without you was something I was not prepared for. I planned for almost every contingency, but the one thing I could not plan was a life without you. Every day I doubted if we would ever meet again. Thank God it happened.

"I apologize for never visiting you in prison, but I could not handle losing both Ron and your. Seeing you in that facility would have been too much for my heart, and I was also paranoid that if they did see me, they would try to use me to further get to you and the cartel's secrets. But that was the past; now we're in the future. Whatever it takes, Jim, we will stay together or die together. I will be at your side through thick and thin, and right now, at this very moment, I can see the **revenge** in your eyes. You don't need to tell me more. Let's get these bastards!"

KING

King had been a loyal friend, associate, and at times a fascinating sexual partner. King knew and understood the Marquis Cartel from its height and grandeur to its now limited operation in the Caribbean Sea. El Capo's Cartel, led by El Capo, was a massive cutthroat operation that spanned the entire frontier from Columbia to the Panamanian coast. The new Marquis Cartel did not operate around El Capo's cartel's borders, which did not extend into the blue waters of the Caribbean. There rests the strength of the Marquis Cartel.

King and Jim together began planning the takeover of every island and its ports in the Caribbean. At the same time, David planned the procurement of the necessary arms, intelligence, and shifting of funds to make all their actions invisible to the world. No boat or plane would be able to pass through or transport their goods within their operation. That was their goal, and their operation begins now.

Jim called King and asked him if he would live aboard the Tito IV for an extended period. He needed King's insight as well as his sexual energy to map out a massive but detailed strategy that they must undertake. King was living in a mansion on the island. He asked Jim if he was sincere in asking him to move onboard the yacht with him. King had never lived with anyone before. Jim confessed to King that his heart is now stone, and he chose not to fall in love again. King asked him why have him by his side in such an intimate way if love would not be involved?

Jim was at a loss for words; he had grown to love the style how King operated. But he never truly got to know him. He told King that he just needed a partner who he trusts with his life to reclaim what was lost.

King looked deeply into Jim's eyes, visibly hurt, and said, "I've never let anybody get to know me. I think both of us are taking a risk that could be very dangerous to our future relationship together."

Jim replied, "We've been associates for almost 10 years, and I think it's time we get to know one another. We are going to embark on a mission that will be death-defying, to say the least. We need to know when we take the bullet for one another that it was worth it. I'm willing to take the risk, are you King?"

King thought for a long and hard, and with the softest of tones looking Jim straight in the eyes, said, "I will take a bullet for you to Jim, so my answer is yes."

The next phone call King made was to one of his bodyguards to arrange for some of his items to be moved to the yacht, for he would be staying in the master suite with Jim. Jim found King more intriguing than ever. Maybe his love for Ron blinded him to these qualities in King. During the course of a day, King's personality would fluctuate from this soft and lovable child to a cutthroat tyrant who gave orders without an atom of mercy. He displayed no such respect for life, human or not, and definitely, no respect for those he felt were disloyal to him.

Jim found it enthralling that an individual could have such an alternating personality. Yet he would end up every night curled up next to him in a fetal position as if he were nestled at his mother's teat. As dominant as King was, he was always a bottom—never a top. This was not a topic for discussion. He commanded his organization with extreme force, yet he wanted his body tyrannized with the same amount of power, which was Jim's responsibility every night in the bedroom.

King was truly gifted; he was naturally tactically minded and knew when and where to execute force in compliance with the cartel's operations. He did not pander to the client; that was Jim's job. The clients either obeyed or were handled accordingly. David's job was to strategically identify the most important clients, those who could contribute the most income to the organization now and in the future. This was based on their historical product movement within and out of the organization. Jim handled face-to-face interactions with the clients for obvious reasons. His personality, looks, and communication skills had always contributed in some way to his success but even more so in today's world. He also used some components of King's organization to gain successful insight into each client's operation.

King, Jim, and David were working well as a team. King had always kept a very low profile. As head of the most ruthless organization in the Caribbean, he cannot leave himself vulnerable or identifiable to anyone ever. The Tito IV was suspected to be one of the few known hangouts for King, and it was rumored that it may have been stolen but without any substantial proof. However, it was still watched by all port authorities and the Coast Guard wherever it traveled. King, living aboard the yacht was too high profile, and the exposure it caused made him feel extraordinarily uncomfortable. He truly enjoyed being with Jim, especially on his overnight adventures. Still, no matter where the yacht was located, he felt eyes on him. Staying aboard was not something that made him feel very comfortable.

One afternoon in the man cave, Jim and King had a long discussion about King's reasoning for not wanting to stay on the yacht anymore. King felt more secure and safer on his island mansion, surrounded by his bodyguards and cameras for protection. Not on a constantly moving platform with too many variables out of his control, and King was a man who loves his control.

Jim said, "I completely understood your concerns. Are you still game for some occasional meetings either onboard the yacht or at the mansion with me? If we can do that, things will work out perfectly."

King told Jim it would be his pleasure and kissed Jim on the lips. King then told Jim that he would also continue his travels to the ports of call to review their Caribbean Sea operations. He will also use his organization for support when necessary and bolster their assets' security as they now start to expand the Marquis Cartel.

That night Jim and King made passionate love. Probably the most tender love that the two of them had shared to date. It was not dominating and forceful as before but smothering nonetheless but with affection. And it was marvelous. King had come to know Jim as he truly was. A soft, tender, and kind individual who truly protected those around him. King felt blessed to have met Jim, and both shared this special "sexual love" between them. They both explored each other's bodies all night long, kissing each other constantly, never leaving one another's touch.

The next day King summoned his bodyguard to move some of his personal items back to the mansion. He left some items on board, such as his chains and whips, to use on his overnight visits. After King left the yacht, David joined Jim in the man cave to go over their plans for the upcoming week. They only had small operations for the Grand Caymans, Jamaica, and the Dominican Republic as of now. They knew they had to avoid any ports on the Central American coastline due to El Capo's grip on them.

David suggested that they investigate the port at San Juan, Puerto Rico, as a possible port for expansion. He told Jim there are several import/ export operations at that location, and their reputation may get some new accounts. Jim agreed with his suggestion and instructed Captain John to head the Tito IV to the port at San Juan, Puerto Rico. On the way there, Jim suggested they stop at Turks and Caicos to check their port out, get fuel and resupply. Might as well kill two birds with one stone.

The distance from Miami to Turks and Caicos is approximately 600 miles, and the distance from Turks and Caicos to San Juan is about 400 miles. The total one-way trip is almost 1,000 nautical miles. It would take them approximately 60 hours to get to Turks and Caicos from their island. And when they leave Turks and Caicos, it would take them about 40 more hours to get to San Juan, Puerto Rico. Jim told King that he would keep him updated as to their location for security reasons during their trip.

The following morning, the Tito IV crew untied the yacht from the pier and set out for Turks and Caicos island. The new team was anxious for the long trip, for this was their maiden voyage on the yacht since being employed. Jim and David sat in the man cave enjoying a 360° view of their surroundings as the yacht hit the Caribbean Sea's blue waters.

There were several small islands that they were going to pass on the first leg of their trip, each beautiful and unique. You could run into beaches with sands of every color, from black to pink. Others were made of rock; some of the islands had coves, while others were dense with forestry. After a while at sea, David began to get tired and told Jim that he would retire to his cabin to take a brief nap.

With David gone, Jim moved forward with a drink in hand and joined Captain John on the bridge. He was instantly astonished by all of the electrical equipment that the yacht was equipped with. Jim thought, *Did we always have all this much equipment, or did King update us for security?*

Jim was also duly impressed by Captain John. He was standing peering into the horizon stoically in his freshly pressed white above-the-knee shorts with his white captains' shirt slightly opened, exposing a tank top. His hairy chest peeked over the cut out of his tank top, and his white cap sat neatly on his head, covering his raven black hair. The bulge in his shorts was so noticeable that Jim's eyes could not avoid staring at it. Jim thought, *Where has John been all of these years, and why on God's green earth hasn't he noticed this fine specimen of a man before today?*

Jim sat down next to John in one of the Captain's chairs. He looked out over the blue water of the

Caribbean and once again wondered why he hadn't noticed John's sexy appearance after all of these years. He was a little bit disappointed in himself. After Ron's passing, Jim was whisked away to prison for seven years while John matured into a stately middle-aged man who was almost equal in age to Jim. Captain John was not married and had no apparent lover. He was very professional and never made any sexual overtone towards any of the crew. Jim wondered how he controlled his sexual appetite being around such handsome individuals while looking rather gorgeous himself.

Captain John turned to Jim and said, "We have clear seas for the next hundred miles, so I think now is a good time for an emergency drill. What do you think, Jim?"

"It sounds like a good idea to me. We need to get our weapons out of storage, cleaned and prepped anyway. We can't be caught with our pants down just because this is technically our territory. Look at what happened in Panama."

Captain John nodded and set off the emergency alarm on the yacht. Within a few minutes, each crew member, along with all of the passengers aboard, reported to their staging area along with their weapons ready for inspection by Jim and the Captain. It was a good idea that Captain John suggested that this training exercise. The new crew members did not quite understand the proper procedures in loading and positioning themselves for a defensive stand. Both Jim and Captain John questioned if they had ever fired a gun during their training.

Jim summoned Timothy, Andrew, and Stephen to the man cave. He instructed them to go over the emergency procedures with the new crew members and have them practice shooting their rifles off the yacht's stern to ensure they both knew how to operate their weapons and hone their accuracy. Jim told them that we would have another drill before they got to San Juan and ensure that everyone was properly trained.

CAPTAIN JOHN

*A*fter twenty hours at sea, Jim told Captain John to pull up to one of the small, deserted islands and anchor. This way, all of the crew could take a break while Chef Jeff prepared a beautiful dinner for them all. Jim asked Captain John if he would have dinner with him in the man cave while the rest of the crew had dinner in the main dining room. Captain John was delighted to be invited to the man cave where he had rarely been on an informal basis. Keith served both of them dinner in the man cave. The menu consisted of grilled salmon with a white sauce, sautéed green beans with carrots, a mixed green salad with blue cheese dressing with hot rolls, and a carrot cake for dessert. Chef Jeff outdid himself on his first big meal at sea.

Jim and John leisurely enjoyed their dinner as well as each other's company. Keith served them a tasty white wine to pair with their meal and continuously filled their glasses. This led them to finish their fourth glass, where both Jim and John felt no pain to carry on as a carrot cake was served. When Keith brought the desert, Jim asked him to clear the plates and told Keith that he would summon him when additional service was required. Keith understood that the boss did not want to be bothered any further and made himself scarce. Jim and John got up from the table after dessert and relaxed on the Italian leather couch across from them. When Jim sat down, he made sure his body came in physical contact with John's muscular hairy leg and quickly evaluated John's reaction.

John responded by putting his hand on Jim's crotch and said, "I've been wanting to do this for over ten years. What has taken us so long?"

Jim replied, "Until now, I wasn't available. How long are we going to be anchored here?"

"I thought we could take about an hour's break. So, we got a little over an hour to stroll down to your cabin and get to know each other."

Jim got up and took John by the hand down the Captains' steps that lead from the man cave directly to his cabin, bypassing all of the yacht's public areas. As soon as they both walked through the door, John grabbed Jim and threw them on the bed. The door then slammed shut behind him as he looked at Jim with searching eyes and a slight grin.

"Jim, for the next hour, don't think of me as your employee. Think of me as your Captain."

Still on his belly, Jim looked back at John, who slowly began to take off all of his clothes. Almost immediately, Jim's eyes nearly rolled out of his head. Despite Jim being a few years shy of 50, his dick became as hard as a block of steel just by looking at him. John was extremely handsome. A black hairy chest, massive armpit hairs, thick pubic hairs, his legs were beautifully hairy, and his dick was uncut and enormous. Jim didn't know quite yet what was going to happen and instantly took off his clothes which revealed his hairless chest, slightly hairy armpits, blonde pubic hairs, hairless legs, and a cut dick that was semi-aroused.

Jim turned his body horizontally, laying on his stomach, presenting himself, and said, "What are you waiting for?"

John walked over and grabbed Jim by the waist. He rolled him over on the bed so that the back of his head was buried in the pillow. He got on top of Jim and smothered him with his body, allowing all of his hairy chest and body features to tantalize Jim. As John kissed Jim's lips, neck, and ears vigorously, he then planted a huge hickey on Jim's neck. Jim wiggled with pure delight as John reached Jim's nipples, which he sucked and trolled his tongue around. Jim moaned in pleasure and pleaded for more. As John began kissing Jim's stomach on the way to his pubic section, Jim's dick became fully erect. It was so sore because it had not been this engorged in such a long time, and its skin was stretched beyond its normal size.

John teased Jim's dick by kissing around it and swallowing his balls, allowing his dick to stand above his forehead. Once John felt that Jim was fully erect, he swallowed him down his throat, grabbing his ass and forcing his way all the way down without gagging. He left it there for a great length of time, and Jim had never experienced such a feeling in his life. Jim thrust it in and out of John's mouth so vigorously he climaxed within minutes. Jim was shocked as to the speed and intensity of his climax. Jim was surprised that John was so good in bed.

Jim wondered how he was ever going to compete with John, let alone satisfy him. It had been a long time since he had experienced such a lack of confidence in the bedroom. John wasted no such thoughts and began to kiss Jim vigorously without stopping for a single breath of air. His tongue invaded Jim's mouth and laid siege to the back of his throat with such thrusts that Jim gagged with pleasure. Jim rolled over and begged John to just fuck him. John's dick was massive, and Jim was unsure if he could even take it all. But he was willing to try. John was such a magnificent sexual Titan that Jim wanted to satisfy him no matter the cost.

He told Jim, "Most people can't take it. Are you sure you're okay with me fucking you?"

Jim rolled over and shoved John's dick in his mouth, getting it all wet and sloppy at the same time mentally sizing that thing up to prepare himself for what was coming. Jim then spat out his dick and said, "o for it… I want it all!"

John then put Jim on his back with his legs in the air while looking him straight into his baby blues. He then put his hands around Jim's neck and inserted his massive head into Jim's manhole with a big glob of spit on the end of it to help slide it in. Jim looked into John's eyes and smiled as he experienced both pleasure and pain perfectly married together. John proceeded to insert his complete manhood into Jim without any rejection of its colossal length or girth.

When he was completely in, Jim reached up and grabbed his neck, pulling him down to kiss him, and said, "Fuck me like a slut!"

As Jim began to moan in pleasure, under his breath, he said, "I could love you, if only I were capable." They went at it for over an hour, and after they both had taken a shower, they retreated to the man cave without the crew ever suspecting a thing.

David came up to the man cave after he finished his nap and said, did I miss dinner? Jim told him, yes, but chef Jeff had set-aside his dinner, ready to be served in the dining room at his leisure.

David said, "I think I'll go down now and have my dinner; I'm quite famished." He made his way to the staircase. Just before heading down, he paused, grasping a wooden pillar, and asked Jim, "Did anything interesting happen while I had my forty winks?"

Jim looked at the Captain, smiled, and said, "Oh no, nothing to write home about." David shrugged and then proceeded to go down to eat. Captain John told Jim that he must excuse himself now for he has to attend to the yacht once more and left to pilot the Tito IV.

Jim made his way over to the bar and made himself a scotch and soda. He walked back over and sat down by himself on the sofa, looking out at sea. He continued reliving the sex he had just experienced with a man he was so close to over the years but yet so far. He couldn't begin to explain the satisfaction that he felt within his body. It was the best sex that he had in years. The sex was extremely fulfilling yet tender. Jim was afraid to call it loving, for that term was something he wanted to avoid. He honestly had to admit that he was looking forward to the next roll in the hay with John.

TURKS AND CAICOS

*O*ver the PA system, Captain John announced that they were twenty minutes out from Turks and Caicos. He had called in for a docking assignment, but they had no available 150' foot slips available. Captain John then asked if they had a 200' or 250' foot dock readily available, which they did not. The Harbormaster informed the Captain that he would have to take a mooring in the harbor until a dock became available. Captain John requested that the harbormaster dispatch a harbor boat to guide the Tito IV into the mooring that would accommodate the 150'yacht. The Harbormaster confirmed the request, and Captain John was ready to maneuver the yacht through the complicated course of entering the harbor at Turks and Caicos.

Once moored, Captain John requested a fuel boat to be dispatched to top off for their 60-hour trip to

San Juan. He also asked the caterers' names used by the local yacht owners to restock their supplies while in the harbor. Their phone number was relayed to Chef Jeff so he could order the necessary items to replenish the commissary. After the yacht was tidied up and all the laundry was complete, the staff was granted shore leave for the rest of the day, but they needed to be back on board by 9 PM that night, which allotted them about 6 hours of free time. At 10 pm, JP and George were not on board. Jim asked about their whereabouts to Keith and if he knew what they did during their shore leave? Keith's reply was that once they had reached land, they took off, and he hadn't seen them since.

Keith was not that concerned due to the town's small size. He felt that it was just about impossible to get lost there; however, he was mad since they were neglecting their duties and making the rest of the crew look bad.

By midnight that night, they still were not aboard the yacht, so Jim placed a call to the local authorities to alert them about their missing crew. He gave the local authorities their names, physical descriptions, and his phone number telling them that he would supply them with any additional information if needed to track them down.

The next morning, JP and George were still not to be found. Captain John had planned to depart for San Juan by 10 AM but had to scrub their planned departure. Jim became increasingly alarmed, for he had not had anything like this happen to any of his crew members in all the time since he been at sea. At 1 PM, Jim received a phone call from an unavailable number on his cell phone with no Caller ID. The caller at the other end of the line told Jim that they had JP and George and wanted four million dollars by 6 PM, or both of them would be executed, decapitated, and fed to the sharks as chum. They told Jim not to involve any authorities, or as soon as they caught wind of it, both of them would be killed.

Jim informed the kidnapper that he did not have that type of cash available at this random location and that it would be impossible to get that amount in just four hours.

"I've seen you accomplish the impossible, so don't bullshit me!"

The line then went dead. Jim had now less than four hours to handle the situation, or JP and George would be executed. Jim discussed the situation with Captain John and David. He asked their opinion on how to proceed with this ransom. David found it odd that the kidnappers knew Jim's private line. There has to be an inside man somewhere, either in the police station or on this boat, because how else would they know your private line?

Jim told David to pull their personnel files while he made a call. David started to mull over the data, stitching it together and reading it back to Jim, starting with the beginning when they had moored at Fort George Cay. JP was from Grand Turk, while George was from Salt Cay.

David said, "That's funny; they both are from Turks and Caicos."

When Jim ran their background check, nothing came up on them, so he wondered what link this small island may have to do with the current situation they're in today. He put a call into King and explained everything that had gone on since they arrived and that he had less than three hours to gather up 4 million dollars to save his two crew men's lives. Jim explained how he did not know what the hell was going on and how things looked very fishy.

King contacted the resources that he built at the prison from where Jim was just released. He discovered that a man named Heath, who Jim had sex with, cooked up this plan with someone who knew him in prison and then pointed him to another person who knew yet someone else. This web of people helped paint out a picture of what was going on. They said Heath was from Fort George in Turks and Caicos and was recently released from prison two months ago.

They further told him that Heath had done his homework and collected all the information on Jim that was necessary to know that he was part of the Marquis Cartel's upper echelon and that his floating office was the Tito IV.

King went on, "Heath intentionally got a job working at the yacht club at Fort George using the contacts he made, and he probably waited, hoping that one day he would either run into you or hear the name of your yacht somewhere else and move there. By chance, when he heard the name of your yacht requesting permission to enter the harbor, he took every liberty to check it out. Then he kidnapped these two crew members and interrogated them until he knew that you were on board. He knew that you have an unlimited amount of money. Heath felt that you would never know that it was him behind the hostage situation because he promised to pay those who helped him for their information and silence. But the very contacts and information highway that he used to get to you led directly back to him."

Once again, King had saved Jim and this time in less than 2 hours. Jim felt so indebted to King that he did not know how he could ever repay him. Their relationship was so complicated with the sexual relationship and then the business end of things. He just allowed himself to go with the flow with King. When King wanted it, he could have it. What didn't help the matter was that Jim enjoyed their complicated relationship to the fullest. King told Jim that he needed to make another phone call and he would call him asap. When King got back to Jim, he further explained to him all of the details. Jim asked King if he had resources in the Turks and Caicos to handle the situation.

King said, "Of course! Why do you think I put you on hold for? My men are on the hunt as we speak. Give them an hour... they'll take care of it before 6 o'clock."

Jim waited patiently for any news, and at five-thirty exactly, JP and George arrived on board the yacht. They must have been in a brawl by the looks of things but were now safe and sound. Jim thanked King's men and called him again to let him know the good news and to thank him again. King told him that Heath and three other men had kidnapped the two but were all dealt with accordingly.

King was only disappointed that he could not personally do this favor for Jim. Jim thought how sweet

King was before realizing that King just wanted to kill somebody and say that it was in the name of love. As if he ever needed an excuse. After the call, Captain John pulled the yacht out of the harbor and positioned the throttle to full speed as they headed to San Juan, Puerto Rico. They began a 60-hour trip to complete their almost 1,000-mile journey to inspect yet another potential company to add to their business portfolio.

After they were well at sea, Jim placed yet another call to King to set up something special for him the next time they met. Jim asked what he wanted, and King told him that he owed him nothing.

"That's what family does; they look out for one another. So, how's your trip going?"

Jim replied, "Next time, I think I will take you along with me because we always seem to miss one or the other. It's quite clear how much I need you by my side."

King chuckled and said, "Jim, I miss you far more than you can ever miss me."

Jim smiled and said, "I may not understand our relationship, my dear friend, but I am ever so happy that I have you in my life."

"Jim, I can't be too soft because I got to be a hard criminal 90% of the time, and I don't mean down below. I still have operations to run, and my men are constantly popping in and out, and I don't need them hearing me flirt with you, pretty boy. I got a devil of an appearance to maintain, don't you know."

Jim laughed and said that they would talk later and hung up. King held the phone close to his heart for a moment before hanging up.

SAN JUAN, PUERTO RICO

The 150' Tito IV proudly pulled into the San Juan Bay Marina 100+ hours after it left Marquis Cartel's private island off of Miami, Florida. Captain John and his crew side tied up the yacht in the marina and immediately hooked up the power and the lines. They were all hopeful for a nice relaxing stay in Puerto Rico. Their trip down had been a little exhausting, to say the least. It was time to unwind and get on with the business at hand. David and Jim began by assessing all of the import-export companies in San Juan. They were looking for smaller companies with zero connection to El Capo's cartel or their routes.

Their due diligence paid off, and they identified eight companies that could be of interest. During the day, Jim would scout the companies and their locations out and then assess their business volume by visually assessing each company's daily container operations.

Then Jim will meet with the owners to further get a feel for the organization. If Jim is so inclined, he would then make an offer to purchase. In total, Jim and David estimated that they would be in San Juan for a minimum of two weeks to complete their analysis and purchase transactions. Jim called King to update him on their status and let him know where he could now meet them.

After they reviewed each of the eight companies, Jim decided that only two would be worthy of their purchase. Jim and David half formulated a plan of action but waited until King arrived on board before finalizing their strategy to purchase each company. King's organization was stationed around each location; just in case, the seller refused to accept Jim's offer. Both companies were eventually purchased, one through standard means and one through King's network.

While King was on board the yacht, he and Jim spent several glorious nights together. As usual, Jim dominated King, and with each passing night, his rule grew. King begged for more; he wanted Jim to come up with harder ways of disciplining him every night. Jim found it difficult to be a dominating master, as they call it in the BDSM world, for at times, he just wanted to kiss him and hold him. But King needed it so badly and was so grateful whenever he was controlled and disciplined that Jim could not disappoint him. Jim could never tell anyone what they did in private, for he would never want to insult neither himself nor King. He simply thought too highly of their unique relationship and would never break that trust.

The last night that King spent aboard the Tito IV, he and King were fast asleep after a long night of physical and sexual experimentation. Jim softly began to cry in his sleep. King woke up gently, shaking Jim awake and asking him what was going on.

Jim replied, "I often have these vivid, lifelike dreams or rather nightmares of when Ron was dying. I never could save him, even in my dreams. I still avoid certain areas of the yacht because the memories are still too painful."

King said, "Then why don't you get a new yacht, Jim? You have the money. You need to move on, man. Let go; he would want you to." King held Jim's hand, comforting him, pulling him into his body, and stroking his hair. This was yet again a side of King Jim had never experienced with this incredible man.

Jim looked at King and said, "Well, I guess I just need a solid reason to do it. But I feel like if I get rid of this yacht, I am effectively getting rid of Ron."

"Well, isn't it time to move on, Jim? Don't you think Ron would want you to be nothing but happy and not tortured by this memory?"

"I thought I could handle this memory to keep his thought alive like me naming each yacht after Tito."

King interrupted. "But Tito never died on any of your yachts, did he? No. You took the best and warmest memories of your fallen lover and immortalized him on your yachts. Ron's memory is nothing but pain. It's not healthy. He would want the best for you, and this is not the best for you. "You're right. I just need a little time to process things, but you are right." Jim then grabbed King and gave him a gentle kiss as the two drifted back to sleep, embracing one another.

After all the paperwork and transactions were completed, King boarded a plane and flew to Miami. He then made his way to the marina, where he chartered one of their fast boats to transport him back to Marquis Island, where he had been staying, safe and sound. The Tito IV was refitted for its long journey back to the island. This time Captain John was going to charter a different course, avoiding Turks and Caicos completely and spending more time at sea. With the yacht's fuel capacity, they could travel from San Juan to the Marquis Island without stopping. Jeff made sure that the pantry and freezers of the yacht were fully stocked before their departure. Refueling and restocking the yacht cost almost 20,000 dollars, a sizable sum but consider transporting that many people… that far, for that length of time… the cost was not that high. They departed San Juan on a bright sunny day in mid-September, hoping they could celebrate on the island with all of their family and friends that they have made over the years upon their return.

Captain John set the course needed with the automatic pilot set at 15 knots or 17 miles an hour. They should be pulling into Marquis Island in about two and a half days at that speed, not allowing for any stops, interruptions, or bad weather. The Tito IV had logged over 10 thousand hours on his engines and about 15,500 on the generators. It was time for some major maintenance work on both the engines and generators when they got back to port. The yacht had been so reliable since it was first put into service. The manufacturer had lived up to its reputation as making the best yachts in the world.

Jim had thought about replacing the yacht and remembered the time when he had flown to the Netherlands to pick it out. Maybe when he got back to the island, he would make another trip to the Netherlands and look for a new yacht to replace the Tito IV. For this one had become a little too famous for his liking.

Well underway. Jim reviewed all of the bank accounts that the Cartel maintained from all over the world. Under his control, he had over one hundred million dollars scattered throughout twelve banks. Ron had set them up so when one bank reached a certain dollar amount, it would automatically transfer to another bank, then to another bank, which made it very difficult to trace by any electronic accounting system. Jim even had difficulty putting his finger on the exact dollar amount on any given day. Still, in round figures, he knew the amount was immense and more income was added daily from their operations.

THE TITO V

*J*im placed a call to Jake Goldstein at FEADSHIP Yacht Sales in the Netherlands. Remarkably, Jake's number was still active, and he still headed the sales operation. However, he was not in the office when he called, so Jim left him a message to return his call. The next day Jake contacted Jim and told Jim that he was surprised to hear from him.

Jim replied, "Your yachts are so well-made that they don't wear out. I'm calling to see if you have any 200' yachts on the lot. I'm sure you know my style. My partner was killed, so I'm buying one just for myself. One chapter closes, and I'm ready to start anew. It's time for a larger one and a newer one. I want a mega yacht with MTU 4000 engines. I understand they are the highest powered and most respected engines for these yachts."

"I agree; they are what we recommend for on any mega yachts,, 200' or more."

"If you have any mega yachts available, can you fax me a picture of the interiors? If I like them, I'll fly over and take a look."

"I have three mega yachts for sale. A 210', 225' & 250'. All of them are exceptional, and we custom-build them for other individuals who put deposit money down on them. So far, we haven't been able to close those three deals with the individuals who first commissioned their building. So, as a result of that, there would be substantial savings on all three of them. I'll FAX you the pictures of the interiors within the hour, and you can take a look at them. If any of them interest you, Jim, I'll provide you with more detailed information."

"Sounds like a plan. As soon as I get the pictures, I'll review them in detail and get back to you."

Jim and his crew have been out at sea for several days. During these long days and nights, Jim and the crew had the opportunity to get to know one another. They played cards, watched movies, did rounds of drinks, and had delightful dinners prepared by Chef Jeff. His culinary creativity was always put to the test creating surprise meals out of usually traditional entrées.

Jim let Jeff know that they were open to any creation that he served. They always wanted him to complete the meals so that he could eat with them in the main dining room. It was easy for them all to become as close as family during these long bouts at sea. They were allowed to sleep in the VIP guest rooms when no one occupied them, and Jim didn't ask who was sleeping with who.

All Jim wanted was for them to have a good time and complete their assigned duties. Jim even noticed a change in David. When he came back on board, his rough appearance had now begun to soften back to his original glow. Jim was wondering if he'd hooked up with one of the crewmembers. Jim would not ask, nor did he want to know. All he wanted was for him to be happy. If he wants to tell him or share with him, he will. Jim's sexual encounters with Captain John were more frequent. Jim couldn't resist John. Jim, however, never initiated the encounters.

John just had the uncanny ability to show up in Jim's cabin unannounced, ready for action, and Jim couldn't resist even if he tried. Jim could easily fall in love with John, but he couldn't.

One day when the yacht was on autopilot, Jim stepped in the wheelhouse and asked Captain John,

"What are you doing, showing up in my quarters at all hours of the night?"

"Pleasing you. You're hungry for love. Your body screams for attention. Your soul is empty, and it begs to be filled. And you're afraid to love again. I'm not afraid, Jim, and I will keep showing up until you have either accepted my love or found somebody better than me to fill that void within you. And I will challenge your heart every day. So, what's harder?

Your heart of stone or my steel resolve?"

Jim was astounded and could only retreat to his man cave and pour himself a scotch and soda, a double. He lay on the couch thinking about what Captain John had just told him. It was all true; he nailed Jim to the cross. How did he know all of that without a word from him? He knew Jim is in love with him, and he knows he is afraid to be in love with the Captain, but John is not afraid to be in love with him.

Jim thought that Captain John needs to consider King in all of this. King is the third peg in the wheel. He cannot be eliminated. If John cannot allow King to join in and be part of the wheel and enjoy it, the relationship will never work. King is a permanent part of Jim's life, good or bad, right or wrong; Jim loves King very much in their unique relationship. King could just be in bed with Jim when John walks in, and he'll find out instantly that King is not shy. He'll invite Captain John to join in anytime. Maybe that's what he needs to do. That's what he did with Ron, and it worked out fine.

The following day Jim got several faxes from Jake with pictures of several of the yachts. Jim was duly impressed by the 250' yacht. It had eight master suites and eight crew quarters plus a Captain's quarters, a massive dining room, upper and lower salons, and yes, a 3rd level salon that could be converted to a man cave that was double the size of the current one of the Tito IV. It was powered by two MTU 4000 engines, the largest engines made for mega-yachts. It had three generators and two freshwater systems that could produce up to 1,800 gallons a day. One could go on for hours about the luxury of this yacht because it was simply astounding. Jim called Jake in the Netherlands and said he would fly over in two days and take a look at it.

After Jim arrived in the Netherlands, he boarded the 250' mega-yacht and toured it for about five hours. The only thing that Jim wanted to change was the swimming pool which he said would never be used. He wondered how long it would take to get it converted into a livable space. The Jacuzzi will probably never be used either, but it could stay just for the crew's sake. Jim's idea about the swimming pool was just to board it over and cover it with the same teak flooring that is already there and put four hatch covers in it so it could be used for storage. Jake agreed with that idea and that would be a quick fix.

Another question Jim had was about relocating it to Miami. Jake said they had two options, but cruising it across the Atlantic rather than transporting on a ship would be quicker and cheaper. They can leave the Netherlands and arrive in Miami in about 23 days, considering this yacht's speed and fuel capacity.

Jim thought for a minute and said, "That would be a good break-in cruise for it. Now we gotta talk dollars and cents, Jake. What is your asking price?"

"The original price was $236,000,000."

"That's a little steep, Jake; you wouldn't have called me all this way to waste my time."

Jake said, "True, well now let's talk about the actual price. As I told you, the yacht was built specifically for the client who put down a substantial deposit and could not finish financing the purchase. As a result, I will sell the yacht with the $10,000,000 down payment deducted from it."

"As kind as that is, that deduction won't make a dent in the sales price. As you know, I deal in cash, no financing, no quibbling, just plain old cash. The only condition I have is, just don't deposit the cash in any bank in the United States like you did last time. Jake, I'm going to allow you to give me the lowest price possible before I give you my price. I don't want you to lose out on selling this precious yacht."

"Let's head into my office."

They both got into the company golf cart and sped off to the yacht broker's office. Once inside, Jim was impressed that Jake had updated his office furniture with the most current custom yacht furniture made today. He complimented Jake on his furnishings and asked him if he sells pieces individually.

"Yes, we furnish houses, condos, yachts, cabins, trailers, and RVs. Really, we'll furnish anything that you want, and we will customize the furniture to fit the space. Do you want some different furniture in the man cave?"

"And your company will make it, is that correct?"

"That's correct, Jim."

"I may call you again when I get an idea of what I want. Now let's get down to the mega yacht."

"I can let you have it for $200,000,000. That's our company's bottom line. Nothing lower."

"I'll take it. How do you want to handle the payment, Jake?"

"As before, can you make $10,000.000 down payment in cash right now?"

"Yes, I can handle that, but you have to deliver it to Miami at your expense. I will wire the rest to you from my normal backchannel. Sound good to you?"

"That's fine by me. Now, as far as the pool refurbishing, I'll bill you for that."

Jim replied, "Okay, so it sounds like we're all settled then. When can we expect to get it?"

"It will probably take about one week to convert the pool area. I'll have them start on that immediately, and then it will take about 23 days to cross the Atlantic, so that is about four weeks minimum."

"Why don't you call me when you are a week out so I can make arrangements for my crew to be in Miami to receive it. Do you have any interest in taking our current yacht as a trade, or do you want to sell it for me?"

"How much do you want for it?"

"I have no idea; that's your business."

"When we deliver the yacht to Miami, we can take a look at yours and evaluate the sales price."

"Sounds okay to me," Jim replied.

Jim flew back to Miami and then transferred to Jamaica to head to the Royal Jamaican yacht club where the Tito IV was currently docked. When he got on board the yacht, pandemonium ensued. There was a problem with one of the businesses that they brought in Puerto Rico. Apparently, one of their clients caught wind of the change in ownership and refused to ship through their organization. Jim got on the phone with the manager and asked who the client was. The response was someone related to El Capo. Jim took a deep breath and said to himself, *I don't want to get involved with that asshole again.*

Jim called King and told him about the situation in San Juan. King was quite aware of the client and his relationship with El Capo's cartel. "Jim, just hang loose, and I'll call you back when I have a plan of action in place."

"Okay, it's in your hands now."

Again, Jim was indebted to King. He knew King would handle the situation no matter how big or how small the problem was. Jim had complete faith in him. Over the years, Jim has developed this lasting relationship with King that's both emotional and physical but all business at the same time. King and his organization protected Jim and all his people and kept the Cartel functioning with muscle. At the same time, Jim could never turn his back on King's emotional or physical needs. Despite King's inability to allow himself to be even slightly emotional, he dearly loves Jim and has proven that fact many times in a number of ways. King's love for Jim does not stand in the way of his organization. King uses his organization's might to demonstrate his hardened and direct love for Jim.

It's a complicated relationship.

Three days later, the San Juan port manager called Jim and said that all of your station's ownership issues have been resolved. The client and his shipments are flowing as usual with no comments. This took a weight off of Jim's shoulders because he did not want to deal with any problems with El Capo's Cartel this early into his plan. He called King to ask how he handled the problem in Puerto Rico.

King said, "Don't worry about it; there's nothing for you to worry about. All you need to do is concentrate on the other businesses and make sure they are as successful as possible. I'll handle all the dirty work. If there's any other business that you need help with, just give me a call."

KING'S LOVE

*J*im invited King to the yacht for dinner, and King graciously accepted. Jim told King that he had missed him and needed to feel his body next to him.

King laughed. "You need to feel my body next to you. Well, I need to feel your body in me. See you tonight, Jim; I'll be there between six and seven. I'll check the schedule right now with my 'to go boat' and bodyguards. Jim said, you know when we get our new yacht, we are going to have so much more room for not just us but your bodyguards as well, so they'll have their own place to stay when you spend the night with me."

Jim paused for a moment and told King that they needed to have a talk about Captain John when he gets there.

"Why?"

"We'll go over it when you get here. King, have a safe trip tonight."

King arrived early at about 5:25 PM. That was highly unusual for him. He's either exactly on time or a little late, never early. Jim guessed that he was just anxious to see him. King was dressed very casually today, which was quite different from his usual rough and tough appearance. He didn't have on any baggy pants with his ass showing, no tank top or bulletproof vests. King was wearing some nice pants with a dress shirt and deck shoes with no socks. His black hair was combed, and he even had put on cologne which he never wore. He always said that was sissy stuff, and a guy like him, out in the field, can't wear that sissy-smelling stuff. He looked more handsome tonight than he ever looked. He appeared very soft and appealing. No one would ever guess that he was the leader of the notorious Jamaican Cutthroat gang.

Jim was anxious to go to bed with him because he had different intentions than the usual S&M activities. Jim asked Chef Jeff if dinner was ready to be served. Jim was anxious to proceed to bed and explore King's innermost secrets that he was signaling through his appearance tonight.

After dinner that night, King immediately grabbed Jim's hand and led him to the master suite of the yacht. When they got inside, King slammed the door shut and undressed Jim, which he never did. King ran his hands gently over Jim's body and kissed his lips softly. He then proceeded to Jim's neck and then to his nipples with vigorous sucking and biting foreplay. Jim could not control his erection. King laid Jim on the bed and continued to caress his body, kissing it, and bypassing his erect penis, going down his legs until he reached his feet. He took Jim's feet one by one in his mouth and washed his toes with his tongue until they were wet with spit. Then he raised Jim's legs in the air using both of his hands and proceeded to kiss both of his legs until he reached his manhole. King spread Jim's legs apart and went headfirst into his dark cavern for such a long period that Jim just melted with pure delight. His relaxed manhole felt like it was a cave while King's head was buried deep in it. Then King kneeled next to the bed, and before him stood Jim's penis fully erect and surrounded with blonde pubic hair which was begging to be swallowed in its entirety.

But King had other things in mind as he raised Jim's legs above his shoulders. King's erect penis, surrounded with mounds of thick black pubic hair, was now scraping Jim's ass. King was now preparing for his penetration of Jim's manhole for the first time since they had known each other.

King's gentler side was like a stranger in Jim's bed. Jim reached up and kissed King, not sure what King's reaction would be. King responded with a kiss so sloppy and loving that Jim didn't know exactly what to do. King gently inserted his enormous penis into Jim's manhole for the first time. King did it without lube or spit, just natural pre-cum that covered the head of his cock as it slipped in without a grown or a moan from Jim. Jim reached up with his arms around King's neck, pulled him down, and kissed him as King fucked Jim with all his might until he climaxed within a short time.

After he climaxed, he withdrew his penis and collapsed on top of Jim. And with exhaustion, King said, "I love you with all of my heart. You have humbled me as no other man could, and I lay before you as a man that is all yours. I want you with me for the rest of my life. I don't want to live without you."

Jim was so humbled and felt true love for the first time in his life. A love even greater than Tito or Ron, and that was saying a lot. Jim thought he would never experience a deeper love than Tito's, but what he experienced today with King eclipsed even that. Jim hoped Tito would understand Jim's deep love for King. Jim thought he would never love again, and to his surprise, the man he fell for was King, who just unlocked his heart. *Who could be better to love? We are both **marked for death**.*

Jim told King, "I've loved you for a long time. I have controlled my emotions only to ensure that I pleased you to the degree you wanted. My life has always been in your hands physically, but now you have me emotionally too. I'm yours if you will have me, for I want you."

King rolled over and told Jim, "Take me. I'm all yours."

Jim satisfied himself while satisfying King in a way that they both understood, for no others needed to know or understand but them. King's Cutthroat gang is one world that Jim needs not fully understand, only to accept. The person who leads that organization is his lover, a kind and loving man who is understanding and protective. Who, without exception, is his soulmate for the rest of his life. Together they have achieved this climax through the many experiences in their life that others were fearful of exploring. Only King and Jim exist in their world of the Marquis Cartel, which they are now rebuilding to its former control of the Caribbean Sea.

They relocated all of the financial and accounting records for each of the import/export offices and the managers to the island mansion. Jim and King agreed that the yacht was too well known in the Caribbean Sea, it was not a safe place to store the records. The island mansion was a far better place for its safekeeping. Planning, execution of audits, and controls could still be performed on the yacht, but results of those reviews and any records of monies received or transferred would be maintained on the island.

The Tito V arrived in Miami 60 days after the purchase date. Jim told the crew they would be responsible for transferring all items from the Tito IV before they departed Miami on the Tito V. He also informed them that the yacht's exterior color was black with metallic silver lines through it as well as the interior colors so they would recognize it.

The new yacht would not be named; they would be traveling incognito throughout the Caribbean Sea. He asked Captain John if he would need a trial run with the new yacht to understand the new MTU 4000's controls before they set out for Marquis Island. Captain John assured Jim that the yacht was only 100 feet longer than Tito IV and the engines were the MTU 4000's, and he was familiar with them. Captain John felt comfortable that after they were fueled and all of the personal items transferred, they could take off for the island without delay. Jim instructed Captain John to have Chef Jeff and Chief Steward Keith outfit the yacht's pantry to capacity so that they can set out immediately.

After a short cruise from Miami, the Tito V deckhands secured the new yacht to the pier at Marquis Island. The Tito V stood ready for departure. The date, December 1st, 24 days before Christmas, and what a Christmas it's going to be.

The Tito V was almost indescribable. The floor plan of the new yacht was almost identical to the Tito IV but 100' larger. The new yacht had four additional VIP staterooms, one more owner suite, and four additional crew rooms that slept four more crew. The galley was larger, as was the main salon. They did a wonderful job of removing the swimming pool and covering it with teak flooring, which added extensive space on the lower deck for social gatherings surrounded by a black onyx bar. The black and silver interior coloring was so rich and stately, it was hard to imagine that you were indeed on a yacht rather than a mansion on any island in the Caribbean Sea.

Jim asked Chef Jeff to contact the "Caterer to the Yachts" and have them prepare the Christmas Eve and Christmas Day's brunch and have it transported to the yacht and stowed away in our refrigeration units as appropriate. He also said they might as well begin the preparations for New Year's Eve and New Year's Day. Chef Jeff asked if Jim had a preference for the meals.

"No, you go ahead and select the meals; you do such a fabulous job." Jim also had Chef Jeff ask the "Caterer to the Yacht's" for staffing so that he and the rest of the crew could have time off. Jim informed the crew that they could bring guests aboard the yacht for the Christmas Eve and Christmas Day dinners as well as the New Year's Eve and New Year's morning brunch. However, the crew would still have to report back to work by 6 PM New Year's Day.

Christmas Eve, the crew and their guests, along with Jim, King, and David, were all on the back deck of the Tito V. It began to rain, so everyone moved into the main salon when one of the crew members said, "I'll be the bartender for the night. What will everybody have to drink?"

Jim told him to "make mimosas for all of us; it's an easy drink to make and goes down easy."

"Mimosas it will be."

They drank bottles and bottles of the finest champagne. At the stroke of midnight, Jim got up from his chair and asked Chief Steward Keith to go to his stateroom and bring up the box from the foot of his bed. When Jim got the box, he began by calling off the names of every person who lived or worked on the yacht. The most magnificent gift that he bestowed on anyone that night went to King. It was a massive, very butch, ruby and diamond ring encircling the second and third finger on his left hand. Only a macho man would ever dare to wear this ring, engraved with the special date when they committed to each other. The remainder of the gifts were cashier's checks in various denominations according to the individuals who were of personal service to Jim. Jim used discretion in his definition of personal service. There were only a few that stood out among his guests, including Captain John, who received the largest cashier's check, and the three leaders of the Black Disciples who came all the way from Panama. The final check went to David, who has been by Jim's side for many years.

THE RE-BIRTH
OF THE MARQUIS CARTEL

*A*fter the New Year's celebration was over, King and Jim sat back in the mansion on the island and started to plan the re-birth of the Marquis Cartel. Kings' organization had grown to over a thousand gangsters throughout the Caribbean Sea. His Cutthroat operation was feared by even the local police on every island that the Marquis Cartel had their ports of call. King assured Jim that it was time to use the muscle that his organization had bolstered to bring shockwaves through the import/export business in every port and in every country the Caribbean Sea touches.

Jim was in total agreement with King. He was tired of playing it by the rules; he was going to play it like El Capo's Cartel but even worse and more ruthless. Jim was not going to let that little weasel El Capo threaten his new business as he did in the past. This time the Marquis Cartel would reign by the numbers and disintegrate any organization that stood in the way of their new savage empire. It's time to put King's face on the front page of our Cartel. Up until this point, he had been a silent partner that only supported Jim's operations. Now he is the organization and will be the one who is in charge of all of the ports of call throughout the entire Caribbean operation.

King will let it be known through his lieutenants that his gang is now in control of all of the Caribbean Sea clients, and they are doing business with King of the Marquis Cartel. If any port from Venezuela to Panama wants to ship their products via water or air across the Marquis Empire, they will have to get permission from King's organization. There will be no easy challenge. But no one can stand in the way of King's organization because they hold all of the power.

The radar mapping installed on the Tito V combined a network of radars. It was so powerful that it could identify flights originating anywhere from Brazil to Panama heading to Miami, crafts headed from Europe, the East Coast of the United States, and any port in the Caribbean Sea. Once King identified them, ground-to-air missiles would shoot them out of the sky. Seagoing vessels originating out of those ports were identified on the same radar. "Go-fast boats" in vast numbers could be dispatched to destroy El Capo's shipments before they ever reached their destination. El Capo and his related organizations could not battle with King's organization on the waters or in the air of the Caribbean Sea.

Once again, the Marquis Cartel is dominating the drug business in all ports of the Caribbean Sea. This time it's being managed differently. King's Cutthroat operation is the front line of the cartel. If any port from Panama to Venezuela wanted to move products, they needed to contact King's organization to arrange their product shipment. His percentage rate increased to 45%, and the new Cartel's revenue was so huge that David was having a difficult time manipulating the accounts. David's job was to prevent the accounts from showing a daily balance to indicate any signs of money laundering and tax evasion in the United States legal system.

David and Jim worked tirelessly on the books of the cartel. David flew to various countries in Europe, opening up additional accounts to offload money to not draw the suspicion of the DEA or the IRS. King maintained his cut in cash and paid his network that he had established over the years in cash. He maintained a network of trusted runners that delivered the money. His mansion on the island contained so much cash that you could not count it all in a year. When King had the mansion constructed, he installed underground vaults with secret passageways that only he and a couple of trusted lieutenants could gain access to. He did not even share that information with Jim. Not that he did not trust Jim; Jim had his fortune, and he and King had yet to intermingle their funds.

The El Capo cartel tried vigorously to outrun and outfly the Marquis Cartel almost daily. King had the radar systems manned 24/7 to ensure nothing got past their security points.

Jim told King, "Our cartel is raking in an enormous amount of money every month due to the increased percentage that we are charging for the shipments."

One day, David requested a meeting with Jim and King in the man cave. David said, "We can't handle any more money. We will expose ourselves sooner or later because our positive cash flow in bank accounts all over the world has reached its maximum."

"My stash house is running over with cash. By the last estimate, I have over 5,000,000,000 dollars stashed away. My contractors work night and day to expand vaults to meet storage requirements and even converted most of his bills to 100s just to eke out a bit more room. I can't handle any more money either."

Jim said, "Well, what do you think we should all do about this?"

David was first to speak up, "We should curtail our operation for a while until we either find a new place to hide money or spend some of it so our bank accounts could be replenished with new income."

King said, "I guess we have enough money to retire and enjoy life, don't you think, Jim?"

"Maybe it's time to get out of the business. We have been very fortunate. King, if someone in your organization is strong enough to take over the cartel operation and just pay us a monthly 'like rent for the house on the island,' that would keep us flush in spending money. That's the same way we paid Henry Martinez when we began running the business for him. We can put all of our heads together and determine the amount for rent."

David replied, "That sounds like a great idea. Let's retire and be together without all of the stress, killings, money laundering, and the risks we take every day to maintain our current business. Let's let somebody else do it while still receiving an outstanding income because the cartel operation is running above 100%."

King said, "Let's meet tomorrow morning at 10 o'clock here in the man cave. Maybe I can come up with a plan that we can all agree upon that will terminate our current business positions while receiving a monthly rental income."

JIM-KING-JOHN

*J*im knew that he would have to discuss his relationship with Captain John with King sooner or later. Captain John had fallen madly in love with Jim, and it was obvious. While King was on board the Tito V, Captain John avoided all contact with them. Jim and King were entangled in a codependent relationship. They both needed each other to survive, and King trusted Jim in bed. And Jim did everything in bed to earn King's trust. Jim needed King and his warriors to survive the wrath of any person or organization who challenged him. King trusted Jim with his innermost feelings, and he knew that Jim would never betray him.

Jim knew that King was soft and sensitive in his own way, but his way was not so natural. Jim's sexual encounters with King became fulfilling over time. Jim learned how to please King in several ways each time that they were together. On a few occasions,

Jim convinced King it was okay for him to be the dominant one. King's beautiful body was not one to be ignored.

When he used it to pleasure Jim, it was so satisfying that Jim's sexual climaxes were even envied by King. King's strong arms could twist Jim in all directions, and at the same time, he would pleasure Jim in newfound positions that even King himself enjoyed. Jim hoped that King, in time, would be more dominant in bed so they would share the passion of love 50-50.

Jim did not know how to explain Captain John's feelings to King. At some point, he had to share with King that he and John had gratifying sex together. He had to make sure that King knew that it was only sex, not love and passion, as he and King shared each time they were together. Jim wondered every day how to communicate this dilemma to King.

One afternoon King and Jim and their three bodyguards were taking a walk on the sandy beach on the island. Jim had his arm around King's shoulder and rubbed the back of his head with his hand. Jim stopped for a minute and turned to look into King's eyes and said, "King, there is something I need to share with you. Captain John and I had sex before you and I became a couple. He is still madly in love with me, and

I have been having a difficult time handling this issue. How do you recommend that we handle the situation?"

King replied, "Do you trust me to take care of it?"

"Yes, I do, King."

They concluded their walk, jumped into the shore boat and headed toward the Tito V for afternoon cocktails with the residents of the yacht and its crew. When King and Jim returned to the yacht, George, the deckhand, greeted them and helped them board.

"Well, it's so nice to have you all on board this afternoon. What's the pleasure of your visit?"

King was quick to reply, "We just came to check out our yacht."

When King, Jim, and the rest of their guests were all settled in the main salon, he hit the intercom and ordered drinks for everyone. JP, their Stewart magically appeared within minutes with a scotch and soda for Jim and mimosas for the rest of the guests. The Tito V main salon had been expanded to include an additional sofa, 4 swivel chairs, side tables with nautical lights, and a larger 9' x 18' leopard skin rug on the floor. The room's wood was a dark walnut with a silver grain that sparkled when the sun hit it. The room was so impressive that you'd imagine that you were in a five-star hotel. There were two French provincial desks, one on each side of the room with silver-plated telephones on, to conduct a brief business encounter.

After their drinks arrived, King said, "Let's invite Captain John to join us for a drink as well."

"It's all in your hands, King; I will follow your lead," Jim replied.

King dialed the intercom and summoned Captain John to the main salon. When John entered, he saw King sitting proudly in the easy chair next to Jim. Captain John did not know what to do next.

King said, "Order a drink, John; I'll call JP."

King pushed the intercom for service, and JP appeared. King requested another round of drinks and asked John what he would like.

Captain John replied, "A scotch and soda and as I think about it, make it a double."

JP told them that the new round of drinks was on its way, and as soon as he left, King said to Captain John, "I hear you're in love with Jim."

That comment took both Jim and Captain John by surprise. Captain John replied, "Yes, I am."

King replied, "You're a lucky guy; Jim is a worthy person to be loved. But unfortunately, John, I found him first. To satisfy your sexual curiosity, Jim and I are going to invite you to join us in bed tonight, so you can experience some of the sexual bliss that we share. How would you like that, John?"

Captain John replied, "It's better than nothing. Just let me know when and where I'll be there."

Jim looked at Captain John with a satisfying smile on his face, and he knew that everything was going to be okay. When Ron joined in with him and King, Ron enjoyed it immensely. Now a new adventure with Captain John and King will begin. The three of them finished several rounds of drinks in the salon. It was approaching 10 p.m., and they had a good buzz as King got up out of his chair and took Jim by the hand. Then he reached over and grabbed Captain John's hand and led them both to their master suite. The new yachts master suite was gigantic. Its king-size bed was surrounded by sofas with an enormous television mounted on the wall at the foot of the bed. The magnificence of the dark wood with the silver streaks throughout glowed with the dim lighting.

When all three of them were in the suite, King shut the door with a bang and reached over and gave Jim a passionate kiss that seemed to last forever. As he unbuttoned his shirt and stripped him naked, he threw Jim on the bed. King hastily stripped himself of all his clothing and laid upon Jim and smothered him with his rich chocolate body, dark pubic hair, and fully erect penis.

King turned to John and said, "What's your problem, come and join us." John slowly undressed and laid next to Jim on the bed displaying his gigantic manhood surrounded by thick black hair and waited for King's command.

King took hold of Jim and flipped him over between the two of them and said, "Now Jim, get to work and show John what you do to me."

Without hesitation, Jim began kissing King viciously down his neck until he got to his nipples which he then bit so hard that King screamed with pleasure. Jim then took one of his hands and choked King while the other proceeded to his dick and balls, grabbing them and tugging hard. He then pushed his legs into the air and began pounding his hard dick into King's manhole. Thrusting with all of his might, Jim made King groan with every thrust until they both climaxed simultaneously. Then Jim tossed John on top of both of them.

Jim told John, "Show us what you can do and don't be a pussy, give it to us like a man."

John began kissing both Jim and King simultaneously. He did not know which he liked better. King grabbed John by the head and pushed his head down, and face fucked him until just jaws were sore with bliss. King then flipped John on his stomach and attacked his manhole so hard that John begged King to stop. King continued his merciless thrust until he put both hands on John's head and pulled John over on his back. He then slid his enlarged penis into John's mouth that was covered with shit and pre-come. John gasped for air, but King did not let up. Finally, King withdrew, but all John could taste was King's shit and pre-come.

When everything was said and done, King told Captain John, "If your relationship with Jim continues, this will be what he can look forward to, if not worse. Don't underestimate me."

THE RE-BIRTH
OF THE MARQUIS CARTEL ACT II

*J*im placed a call to Jake Goldsmith and asked if he had sold the Tito IV yet.

Jake said, "No, we have not sold it yet. It's in Miami waiting to be serviced and cleaned before we put it on the market."

Jim told Jake that he no longer wanted to sell it. He wanted to put it into dry dock and refit it with all of the newest electronic equipment available.

"While in dry dock, replace the engines with the best upgrade in engines available. Additionally, I would like all three generators replaced with Cummings. If they found any other area of the yacht that needed to be serviced to take care of it and I will pay for it. After which, I'll send someone to Miami to return it to the island."

"What's going on, Jim?"

'I'm not going to sell it; I'm going to keep it as our second yacht."

Once the Tito IV retrofitting was complete, he sent Captain John and one crew member to Miami to pick it up and bring it to the island. Captain

John asked, "Why are we returning the yacht to the island?"

"You'll find out in time."

Jim, King, and David continued planning the power transfer of the Marquis Cartel, further assimilating it into the Jamaican Cartel, formally known as King's Cutthroat gang to which was based in Jamaica. King had two first lieutenants named: Byron and Aaron. They had been with King since he was ten years old. What people didn't know was that King had a crush on both Bryan and Aaron for years. They were the trusted lieutenants that carried out all of King's kill orders in the organization. They both lived on the island in the other house and were deeply devoted to one another. King had never questioned their relationship. As the leader of his organization, his sexuality and the sexuality of anyone else were not discussed under the penalty of death.

He called both Byron and Aaron to the Tito V. When they arrived, JP quickly brought them to the man cave where David, Jim, and King were meeting. King introduced them to David and Jim, even though both knew them vaguely but had never been formally introduced. They were asked to sit down and relax while JP asked them if they would like something from the bar. Aaron requested a beer, and Byron ordered a gin and tonic with a twist of lime. King thanked them for coming so quickly and told them that he was reorganizing his organization. King asked them to rethink the organization's leadership structure to manage the entire Caribbean Sea operations themselves.

King told them that he was planning to retire soon, and he wanted to divide his position and authority up between the two of them. King felt that they were both in a close enough relationship to ensure the new cartel maintains its current level of operation. Both Aaron and Byron were shocked. They never imagined that King would do anything but run the Cutthroat organization, which effectively embraced their no-mercy policy on all individuals or entities marked for elimination.

King told them that their operation would be based on the Tito IV. The yacht has been returned after its retrofitting in Miami with all new state-of-the-art equipment and new engines. King said that he had all new electronic equipment installed. They will be able to identify any incoming boat or aircraft. He will be transferring a portion of Tito V's rocket and mortar arsenal onboard their yacht.

Aaron and Byron finished their drinks and ordered another one. They looked at King in disbelief; they just couldn't imagine what came over him. What could've softened him to the degree that he is willingly giving up his position that he had held for over twenty-five years. King was deeply rooted in all aspects of the underworld in the Caribbean. Both of them wondered how he could avoid detection, and they knew he would need to be protected wherever he went.

Aaron asking King, "What are you going to do?"

King replied, "You'll soon find out."

King got up out of his chair, went over, sat on Jim's lap, and put his arms around him. He told Aaron and Byron, "This is where my future lies. Jim and I are going to spend the rest of our lives together without worrying about killing, money laundering, drugs, the DEA, and turf wars anymore.

We will find a place somewhere in this world where it is safe for us to live our lives happily."

David spoke up, "What about me?!"

Jim said, "You're going right along with us, not to worry."

Aaron and Byron were shocked that King had found a lover. And it was Jim of the Marquis Cartel. How could this have happened so quickly?

King said, "Well, you got a lot of work to do, so you better start planning and get back to Jim and me when you got your new organization figured out. We will both be anxious to see how it all shakes out."

As they left the yacht, Aaron and Byron put their arms around King and said, "Thank you for the trust you have in us. We will carry on the name of the Marquis Cartel with continued strength in the Caribbean Sea."

When Aaron and Byron got back to the house that night, they packed quickly and moved into the master suite on the Tito IV. It was the first night that they shared a bed without worrying about who knew it since they were 12 years old, rolling around naked in the bushes.

Aaron and Byron rolled around naked again, but this time in a king-size bed, allowing each other's body to fully enjoy their partner's complete manhood. They ravished each other with kisses from head to toe. Aaron topped Byron, then Byron topped Aaron until he exploded all over Aaron's hairless chest. Aaron sat on top of Byron's chest and jacked himself off until he came all over Byron's face. Aaron bent over and licked the tasty stuff off his face, neck, and lips, then laid on top of him until they both fell asleep.

A week later, Aaron gave King a call and said they had their plans ironed out and would like to meet.

King said, "Let's meet on the Tito V at 2 PM."

"We'll be there."

Aaron and Byron's plans were quite simple.

"We are going to be headquartered on the Tito IV, and no one will notice the difference in the leadership change. All of the import/ export offices have already been purchased or are managed by the cartel. The Cutthroat gang members that are scattered throughout the Caribbean Sea need not know that you have retired as of yet, as you have always been a mysterious leader during your 25-year rule. Byron and I have communicated all of your requests to our men in the organization."

King then told them, "The Tito V has not been registered yet to any city or country in the Caribbean Sea. At this time, it is a ghost ship, and that's the way we want to keep it. We plan to take the yacht through the Panama Canal and travel the Pacific coast, possibly to the Hawaiian Islands or maybe the Polynesian islands. We will keep searching for that special place that we feel comfortable and safe. We have more than enough money to live comfortably for the rest of our lives. The Tito V is a long-range oceangoing vessel that is built for this type of exploration. We will take our current crew with us, along with an appropriate amount of protective gear to safeguard us in the event of an attack."

Jim suggested that Aaron and/or Byron put a call into Jake Goldsmith, the yacht broker, and have him outfit their yacht with the appropriate number of yachting crew. "Unless you feel comfortable that some of your gangsters would like to perform these yachting duties."

"You do need an experienced captain," King said. "As I think about it, we'll supply you with Captain John, and I will contact Jake to have him recommend a new captain for our yacht."

The first week after the power change happened, no one knew the difference. The Tito V cruised off to the Georgetown Yacht Club in the Grand Caymans. It had two moorings because there were no slips or side ties large enough to accommodate the yacht. Jim, King and David maintained a low profile and stayed on the yacht. At the same time, the newest crew members took the shore boat into town to order supplies and contacted the fuel barge to refuel the yacht.

They stayed at the Grand Caymans for over three months while Aaron and Byron settled in with their new cartel operation. The cartel's monthly dues for the island rent started to flow in regularly. A&B rarely contacted King or Jim with questions. Jim and King knew it was about time to leave for the South Pacific. The Tito's new Captain was named Oliver; he was from the Netherlands and extremely European. Long straight blonde hair, 6'1", thin, polite, and well versed in the maintenance of the MTU 4000 engines that propel this mega-yacht at a cruise speed of 10knts on long voyages. He is comfortable being the Captain, with his 15 years of experience, the Tito V is his third yacht,

By observation, he appeared to be about 35-40 years old. During the days, he busied himself with yacht maintenance and polished the engines as well as the pilothouse over and over again. The crew continually monitored their supplies to ensure that we were stocked up for the long voyage. Jim and the King started plotting the course from the Grand Caymans through the Panama Canal to the Pacific Ocean and up the coast of California. They only had one concern, and that was Panama. The canals' close proximity to the land left the Tito V vulnerable to attack by El Capo's Cartel.

No one in the organization except Aaron and Byron knew that Jim, David, and King lived aboard the Tito V. All the gang members and the outside world believed that they lived in the Marquis Island mansion. They had done everything possible to indicate that they were there. They even hired body doubles to walk the beach at various hours of the day to portray that they live at the mansion. At the end of the fourth month, Jim and King decided it was time to depart the Grand Caymans for their long trip to the promised land. He ensured that the entire crew knew how to work the automatic weapons on board and understood their assigned emergency stations in the event of an attack. The yacht was fully readied for a voyage. George and JP secured the lines from the mooring, as Captain Oliver slowly motored the yacht out of the harbor of the Georgetown Yacht Club into the open seas surrounding the Grand Caymans.

Once at sea, Captain Oliver set a course for the Panama Canal. The Tito V fuel capacity was 4,000 nautical miles. They had more than enough fuel on board to reach the Pacific Ocean before refueling. So that meant they did not have to stop at any port in the Caribbean or the Panamanian area, thus keeping their exposure to El Capo's cartel at a minimum. The new yacht did not display the name of Tito and was so big, black, and sleek that it sailed virtually cloaked in the waters of the Caribbean Sea. King, Jim, and David enjoyed the yacht's outer decks in the open waters, and there was no boat in sight. The yacht salons plus the man cave were so elegant and large that it was a joy to live within its air-conditioned rooms. Jim, David, and King thoroughly enjoyed their lavish lifestyle.

King's appearance changed drastically. From this thuggish character, he transitioned into a GQ man with all the stylish clothes that money could buy. He walked alongside Jim on the yacht with a tender smile on his face and a slight twist in his hip that he had never shown before. His gay appearance was starting to leak out for the world to see. Jim wondered what he had done to King that turned his switch off. He was now a soft and loving individual who no longer wanted to be dominated in bed but chose to participate equally in their relationship.

Captain Oliver suddenly announced that two boats were coming in from the port side about 40 miles out. Through the advanced radar system, they identified them by their speed and size as DEA boats. He let those on board know to be ready for inspection as soon as they arrive. King and Jim did not concern themselves because they had nothing on board that would violate any rules and regulations. King told the crew that he would meet the agents when they pulled up to board. Jim and the rest of the crew would be scattered throughout the yacht to not draw suspicion on any one individual. When the DEA boats got within 100 yards, they commanded the Tito V to stop and prepare for boarding. Captain Oliver followed their instructions, and the yacht set idle in the middle of the ocean bobbing up and down in the waves.

Two agents boarded the yacht and requested King's identification and certification of ownership of the yacht. His ID was processed through their network, and the yacht's ownership showed the title held by the LLC of their corporation. The DEA agents inquired as to where they were going and for what purpose.

King replied, "We're going to the Pacific Ocean and up the coast of California and possibly onto Hawaii."

"That's a long trip."

"Yes, we're on an extended vacation."

"How many people are on board?"

"Ten."

"Everything looks to be in order, have a safe trip." The DEA agents then departed the yacht.

King took a deep breath. He was so grateful that he had cleaned up his appearance from his old Jamaican hood look to this new GQ-looking man. He looked like he would justifiably own and operate such a plush yacht. Jim joined King on the lower deck and said, "Great job, King." He kissed King on the cheek while wrapping his arms around him.

"I think your new polished appearance helped you pull off this DEA inquiry."

King agreed.

David came down to the lower deck all excited and said, "It's about time that we had some luck. Maybe now good fortune will stay on our side."

About 24 hours later, they were queued up for their trip through the Panama Canal. When they had to announce the yacht's name, Captain Oliver said that it has no name and gave its registration number and who the vessel was registered to. At the Panama Canal port, the harbormaster approved their entry into the first dike, one of many during their twelve-hour trip through the canal. At times during that trip, they were within feet of the land on either side. King alerted all ship personnel to be on guard and positioned at their stations. During these periods, they remained heavily armed.

The Tito V motored through the Panama Canal without incident. After finishing the canal, Captain

Oliver announced they had 1,200 miles of fuel left before they had to find a location to refuel. Checking the charts, Captain Oliver identified three locations in Mexico that they could use as a refueling stop to pick up supplies as they headed north. He called Jim, King, and David to the bridge to discuss which port of entry they wanted to stop at to refuel. King suggested stopping at the busiest port, one with the highest population and a good number of supplies, to finish their trip north. King instructed Captain Oliver to call Lazaro Cardenas' port, one of the Pacific seaboard's busiest ports. Captain Oliver said it would be so busy there that they would not even notice our yacht coming and going. King and Jim agreed with his idea and approved of his plan to enter the port.

It took about three hours to get tied up and to the fuel dock at Cardenas. It was extremely busy because it primarily serviced larger vessels. After fueling was completed, they motored the yacht over to the yacht harbor and tied it to a temporary slip. Captain Oliver requested that the harbormaster put him in touch with the nearest resupply store that services yachts in the club. Chef Jeff contacted the resupply store with his grocery list, and the following day several crates of supplies were delivered to the boat. Once the supplies were on board, it took about three hours for them to be stowed away in various areas of the yacht before they could be untied and depart the harbor.

During these three hours, two strangers were walking alongside the yacht, just looking at it. King observed them instantly. He had stayed focused on the camera system on the bridge. It identified any unknown individuals, obviously snooping within a 100-yard range of the yacht. King took a picture of these two individuals and faxed them to GYS security services in Miami. He requested identification of them as soon as possible.

Just before Captain Oliver was ready to depart for open water, a call came in from GYS. The two men in the picture were connected to a Guatemalan Cartel of unknown origin. King instructed Captain Oliver to immediately depart the harbor without hesitation and head for the open seas. King sounded the alarm on the yacht, which meant everybody was to report to their duty station with their designated firearms. As the yacht inched its way out of the marina, everyone stood ready for an attack. Jim told David to make sure he put on his bulletproof vest; he was not going to lose him if they were attacked. Once they pulled out of the harbor, Captain Oliver went full throttle to the

Pacific's open waters. They headed due west for about 20 miles to prevent any watercraft from following them. Then he made a sharp turn north to head up the coastline of Mexico to California. His fuel capacity would enable him to travel the full length of Mexico, reaching California long before he needed refueling.

THE LAST FEAST

Captain Oliver kept the yacht at 20 knots for an extended period. Once the radar showed that no watercraft was approaching from any direction, he reduced the speed to 10 knots which was the yacht's cruising speed. After all this excitement, Jim, David, and King invited the entire crew and everyone living aboard to join them in the third level Salon for a drink to celebrate their exodus to Mexico. Now all they had to do was get out of the waters of this treacherous coastline which should only take them only five hours, then hello U.S.A. What a sight that will be. They decided to stop in San Diego for an overnight stay. They planned to go out to a nice restaurant for dinner before heading up the coast to LA, San Francisco, and wherever else they decided.

When they were about two hours out of San Diego, Captain Oliver phoned the harbormaster for docking instructions to San Diego's marinas. The harbormaster said they had a 220' slip available in the main harbor, and he would reserve it for their vessel. He asked the vessel's name and how long they were planning to stay. Captain Oliver replied with only the yacht's registration number followed by a brief description and that they were planning to be in San Diego for no more than three days. The harbormaster said, "All is reserved, call me when you're ready to enter the harbor, and I will send out a harbor boat to guide you in."

Captain Oliver informed Jim that he had secured a slip in the San Diego harbor for three days, and they should be there within two hours. Captain Oliver guided the yacht safely into the harbor, and the crew tied up the yacht then secured all the lines and cables for power and sewage.

Everyone went to their cabins to get cleaned up, for they were going out to dinner tonight and to have a little fun in San Diego. King and Jim had a little fun in their king-size bed and once more in the shower, and as always, they were both satisfied with their sexual explorations. King had become such a giving lover it was beyond surprise for Jim. It was only a year ago that King only wanted to be dominated. Now, he rarely asked to be dominated, and he is graciously so passionate and loving it is a beautiful experience to behold. Jim and King showered together that evening before dressing for their outing to San Diego.

There were so many of them they had to take two vans to the restaurant they had selected for dinner. The restaurant was quite elegant and served a wide selection of American dishes. They were all sitting at a row of tables with a view of the entire establishment, toasting to their new life adventure. When suddenly, Jim looked up and saw Jonah, his sickening fat cellmate from prison. Jim had sworn to himself that if he ever saw him again, that he would kill him.

Jim grabbed King's arm and said, "We need to talk."

He led King through a row of tables and to the men's restroom in the back of the restaurant. When inside, he told King that one of the restaurant servers was his first cellmate in prison. And that he had promised himself that he would kill him if he ever had the opportunity. That guy had made Jim perform unmentionable sexual acts to survive in prison.

King looked at Jim and said, "I'll take care of it; that's what I do. What is his name?"

"Jonah. He is a fat, ugly guy with a little dick, and he rapes women and men because he can't get sex any other way."

When they left the restroom and walked back to their table, King asked Jim to point the guy out. When King saw him, he knew exactly what Jim meant. The guy is a waste to humanity. The two kept quiet and tried to finish their meals without rousing any suspicion.

Everyone enjoyed their meal and partied late into the night at various clubs around San Diego. Some of the crew and former crew members went to straight bars and some to gay clubs. Around 2:30 AM, one could hear footsteps arriving on the yacht's teak deck and people laughing as glasses were clinking in the bar and booze was still flowing. Jim had gotten back to the yacht quite early as King had remained downtown to stake out his operation. While King was gone, Jim placed a call to Aaron in Jamaica. He asked if his organization had any connections in San Diego. Aaron said he would call them back. Within the hour, Aaron called and told Jim that they had some affiliation with a small gang in San Diego named the "Thunder Boys." It was a small group but very effective and blended well into the San Diego area. Jim asked Aaron if he could have their phone number because he had an issue that needed to be solved. Aaron provided him with the phone number and asked Jim how things were going.

Jim replied, "Honestly, very well besides this one thing. We're on our way to San Francisco. I'll be in touch."

King hung around outside the restaurant until Jonah got off work. He followed him until Jonah reached his apartment, which was only about fifteen blocks away. After Jonah got home, King quietly encircled the apartment to observe the goings-on from within. It appeared that he had several guy roommates or people there. And they all appeared to be very shady. King used extreme caution in his surveillance and returned to the yacht at about 4 a.m.

When he crawled into bed, he encircled Jim with his arms, kissed on the neck and ears, and told him how much he loved him. Jim asked him why he was so late, and King replied that he was taking care of business. Jim knew that it had to do something with Jonah.

The next morning over breakfast, Jim told King, "I'd like to cut off Jonah's dick and balls and shove them down his throat. Jonah humiliated me so badly that I'll never forgive him."

He reminded King that things happen in prison, but he had to survive. He told King that he had no idea that this shadow would come back to haunt Jim from his past. King replied that this had happened to him many times, and that's why he's now looking forward to a kinder, more peaceful future with Jim.

Later that morning, King called the number that Jim had given him for the "Thunder Boys." The person who answered the phone's name was Winston. King introduced himself as the former leader of a Jamaican gang. He said that he got Winston's phone number from its new leader Aaron, and he would like to meet with him to arrange for some assistance in taking care of an issue.

Winston knew immediately what he meant and asked, "When would you like to meet?"

"I'm staying on a yacht in the San Diego Marina, slip number one. Would you like to meet here at about 6 o'clock this evening?"

"It sounds fine with me; I'll meet you there."

Winston arrived at about 5:45 PM with one henchman. JP greeted Winston on the main deck and suggested that his guest remain on the deck with King's crew while he took Winston to the man cave. He was in awe as to the unique details of the Tito V. His first comment was, "It looks like you're doing pretty well for yourself."

King introduced Jim to Winston, "Jim is my partner, and we have been extremely successful in our business ventures. Now we are reaping the rewards of our hard work."

"What was your business?"

"You should not have to ask if you know Aaron."

King began directly with the problem. "Winston, we have a person that we need taken hostage and delivered to us aboard our yacht. We plan to take him out to sea and make sure that he chums the waters after he is brutally castrated. He made my partner Jim's life a living hell while he was in prison, and now it's payback time. We need your assistance to snatch him from where he lives and bring him to us. Then we will depart San Diego, head to the open sea, and take care of our business. How can we arrange this?"

King went over all the details that he knew of Jonah's work schedule, commute times, and address. He said he did not want to involve any of his crew in the snatch and grab operation, but he would handle the rest of it at sea.

"It sounds easy, and if it's easy as you described, we should be able to complete it for $100,000. King said that's a little high, but I will pay that if no one from our organization is involved. No evidence can be left behind that shows he even existed or will be missed in San Diego."

Winston said, "We have connections in about every location in San Diego, and I think we can make this scrub happen."

"How do you want payment?"

"Cash only, half up front, the remainder when he is delivered to you onboard the yacht."

King agreed, excused himself, went below and returned with $50,000 in cash to seal the deal.

Captain Oliver was planning to depart San Diego the following day. He had told the harbormaster that he was going to leave and asked Jim how long they were going to remain in San Diego, for he had to make arrangements for an extension for their dock rent.

"A 250' slip is tough to come by, so please give me some firm guidance so I can take action accordingly."

Jim replied he was not sure when they would depart, but it would be soon, probably within a day.

The following morning at about 3 AM, Winston showed up at the yacht with Jonah tied up in a large wooden crate with a bag over his head. He was attempting to scream, but his mouth was taped shut, his hands were tied, and his legs were bound. It took four people to carry him on board and stash him in the holding room, where they kept all of their supplies for the yacht.

When they were out of earshot of Jonah, King told Winston, "Man, you did that job fast."

"Everything was just like you said. I'll take the other half of my payment and get out of your hair now." King went below and reappeared with $60,000 in cash.

"A little extra for your professionalism."

After Winston left the yacht, Captain Oliver ordered the deckhands and the dock boys to untie the yacht as they headed out the San Diego yacht club due north toward Los Angeles. Captain Oliver asked King and Jim if they wanted him to stop at the Catalina Island's for a few days before they headed into Los Angeles or wherever they wanted to dock. Jim said to head out to the Pacific's open waters and when it's nice and deep…

"Let's idle for a while; we got some business to take care of."

King, Jim, Alex, and Jamison opened the crate and hauled Jonah's body to the yacht's medical room. Before they did that, Jim had prepped the room by spreading plastic wrap all over the operating table, the floors, and the room walls. He did not want any blood to be found anywhere on the yacht. The four of them dumped Jonah's blubbering body on the operating table. Alex, a former combat medic in the Army, produced a collection of scalpels of various sizes and bone saws. Jim planned to cut off his penis and balls and shove them down his mouth as far as he could and let him gag himself to death. This would be repayment for all the times he put his little dick and balls in Jim's mouth and made him gag.

The two crew members put two mouth clamps opening Jonah's mouth and then stripped him from the waist down, revealing his tiny cock and balls. Jim quickly took a large scalpel and sliced off Jonah's penis, then his nut sack. And as Jonas was screaming, he shoved them both deep inside his mouth. Jonah's was bleeding profusely all over the plastic sheet. Jim had to quickly contain all of the blood within the surgical area, so he took clean sheets on the side cabinet and piled them down around Jonah. The trail of blood was absorbed quickly, and his gagging stopped.

Jim did not want to leave anything to chance, so he went above to his master suite and returned with a revolver and shot Jonas twice in the head, right behind his ear. We all know, as with the murder of Mr. and Mrs. Hernandez, those two shots behind the ear are synonymous with an execution. If anybody finds his body and does an autopsy, Jim wanted the world to know that's exactly what it was, a mob hit.

Jonah was then dismembered into little bits and stuffed into several plastic bags. The remaining crew and those living aboard gathered the plastic bags, weighed them down with diving belts or weights. And just before they threw them overboard, they cut a slit into the bag to prevent them from floating back up. Each bag sank quickly to the depths of the ocean, and in Jim's mind, his revenge was now complete.

That night when King and Jim went to bed after the execution was complete, King whispered in Jim's ear, "Dominate me. Dominate me with everything that you got."

Jim was surprised by King's request, but he never failed to please King. He took King's hands, pushed them over his head, and started kissing him with everything he had. He worked his way down from his neck to just above his erect dick and bit his pubic hairs, pulling them out with his teeth. Then Jim circled down to his balls and fondled them with his nose, smelling all of his manhood. He pushed King's legs into the air and slammed his large erect penis as hard as he could into his manhole. King let out a scream which Jim ignored, and he continued thrusting with all of his might.

King said, "Harder, harder," and Jim obeyed.

That night when it was all over, they laid together

in their sloppy mess, wondering why King wanted to be dominated once more. The softness of the recent days had turned back into cruelty.

Jim asked, "Why?"

"I just helped kill somebody. It brought back my past."

CATALINA ISLAND

Captain Oliver phoned the harbormaster at Catalina Island requesting a mooring for the Tito V, a 250' yacht arriving within thirty minutes. The harbormaster gave them three mooring numbers because the yacht size was too large for two moorings in Avalon's harbor. He told Captain Oliver that the harbor boat would meet them and guide them to their moorings. Captain Oliver thought they were lucky it was winter. There would be no way two moorings would be available for their large yacht within the harbor in summer.

Catalina has no onshore power provided, so the yacht would have to run on its energy supply and produce its own water while composting its sewage. It was built to be self-contained for an extended period of time. Chef Jeff had loaded the pantries on their last servicing, so they had a full supply of food onboard.

Would you believe it was almost 12 months since they had decided to retire and travel the world? Once again, the Christmas season was upon them. That meant Catalina was virtually empty of yachts, and the restaurants were closed except for the weekends. Only the grocery store on the island had a limited number of supplies. King and Jim had been together for over 7 Christmases. They had known each other for even longer. Jim was approaching 50 years of age, and King, a young boy at 47.

David was 41 years old, just a young puppy still gorgeous and innocent as can be. During the last couple of years, David seemed to be somewhat attracted to Timothy, their former chef. He and Timothy were the same age and were remarkably similar in appearance. Very GQ and did not flaunt any sexuality. They were just sexual beings who might be straight, bi, or gay. Whatever it was, they seemed to be extremely comfortable with each other. Jim was not one to question.

They all decided it was Catalina Island for Christmas and New Year's. Their shopping had to be completed via phone, and the shippers made deliveries to the island twice a week. Jim asked Keith to be in charge of Christmas decorations for the yacht's interior and exterior. Of course, Chef Jeff was responsible for all of the holiday meals. If he could find a decent caterer, they too could be utilized. David was in charge of the Christmas tree and its decorations. JP and George were responsible for the yacht's cleanliness to ensure that all the silver was polished and the crystal was ready for display. Timothy, Andrew, and Stephen, the former crew members, were put in charge of entertainment and transportation to and from Catalina. Meaning they would arrange for our shore boat to be hoisted down to the water and cleaned. Alex and Jamison were put on clean-up detail.

It appeared that Christmas was going to be grand. The Tito V, or the "Ghost Ship," was truly a remarkable vessel. Nothing matched it in the waters or in any harbor along the way. When they pulled into port, heads turned, and eyes beamed at the black and silver vessel with the sleekest of lines and no name on the transom. That's how it got its name, the "Ghost Ship." It suddenly appeared out of nowhere, dazzling those lucky enough to catch a glimpse and then disappearing like a phantom without a trace and without a name on its transom.

King and Jim's days on the yacht were of total relaxation. They would generally spend the day dressed in their silk robes and slippers, drinking mimosas starting at 2 PM. Then it was time for an afternoon's nap, then a little action in the bedroom, making an appearance at about 6 PM for evening cocktails and dinner at 7 PM. They both used every inch of the yacht, every floor, looking relaxed and exploring the secret passageways where they hid billions in cash to finance the expedition ahead. The yacht had so many undisclosed places on its blueprints a person could spend weeks trying to find the hiding places that King had stashed his fortune. Before they left, King had to relocate the $3.5 billion he had in the accumulated mansion to the Tito V, as King was not going to leave that amount of money behind, for he did not trust anyone except Jim.

Everyone on board spent a relaxing Christmas and New Year's in Catalina. They grew fond of the lack of people on the island. They thought how nice it would be if they could buy this entire island, as they did off the coast of Florida, and forbid people to come there. Of course, they knew that was not a reality. They all got together on the back deck of the Ghost Ship on New Year's Day to decide where they wanted to go next. Was it Long Beach, Los Angeles, Malibu, San Francisco, or Hawaii? Or did they just want to skip all of the big cities entirely and head for a small island in the South Pacific? Everyone came to a consensus that a small, sparsely inhabited island would be ideal.

They studied the charts attempting to locate a hidden island in the South Pacific to call their temporary home. After extensive research, they came up with the islands of Tonga, a collection of islands that are part of the Bora-Bora, Tahiti chain. The people don't lock the doors, there is no littering on their white sandy beaches, and cleanliness is next to godliness.

By a voice count of the crew and staff on board, "Tonga" was selected as their next destination. They will be heading out within the week for a new transpacific voyage to the "Kingdom of Tonga." When the staff left the boat's sun deck, Jim instructed Captain Oliver to bring his navigation charts of the South Pacific and a chart compass to the top deck's man cave.

Jim, King and David met with Captain Oliver, who was asked the maximum nautical range of the Tito V, went when it was totally serviced with diesel. Captain Oliver replied 4000 nautical miles. Jim instructed Captain Oliver to use the compass and set it at 3500 nautical miles and completed 180° encirclement from South America to North America to reveal the locations that the Tito V could travel without servicing. Their main concern was to avoid any cartel-dominated cities or countries and to have a leisurely trip to the South Pacific.

Within the 3500 nautical mile range was the Marquesas Islands. It was 3276 nautical miles from Catalina. Traveling at 10kn would take the Tito V approximately 14 to 16 days to reach the islands. Captain Oliver agreed that these islands would be an ideal location for the first stop on their o to the "Kingdom of Tonga."

THE "GHOST SHIP" IS ON THE MOVE

*T*he Marquesas Islands are the largest and most remote islands of the French Polynesian group, located 852 miles northeast of Tahiti. Captain Oliver's plan was to arrive at the end of January at the island of Fatu Hiva. It has the largest city, and its capital of Taiohap, maintains a fuel dock and yacht servicing, which they would require after their long voyage.

Jim, King and David relaxed in the man cave, with drinks in hand, as the Tito V cruised out of beautiful Catalina Harbor, destined for the French Polynesian islands.

With laughter in his voice, Jim said, "Remember when we wanted to take that leisurely cruise to Panama. We got hit by that hurricane; what an eye-opener that event was. Let's hope this 3400-mile trip is much more relaxing. While we are on this voyage, we've got several days to think about how our business is doing and what we would like to do in the future. It's about time we get out of vacation mode. David, why don't you take and gather up the books? King and I would like to know how the revenue regeneration of our Caribbean operation is doing."

Jim took King by the arm to their massive suite on the bow of the yacht. Once inside, Jim guided King to the plush sofa, located in their suite's sitting area. With all the calmness that he could muster, Jim told King that he had not felt well for the last two months. He went on to say that he felt it was probably that psychological adjustment between their two worlds. But most recently, Jim has noticed increased tiredness and low morale that he had not felt before.

King was immediately alarmed. He asked Jim if his newfound retirement had contributed to this?

Jim replied, "I don't think so. King, we gotta keep this between us for the time being. When we get to the islands, I will see a doctor and get a checkup. How's that for a deal?"

King replied, "Remember, we promised we would never keep secrets from one another. Secrets kill".

"Understood," Jim replied.

During the long voyage, everyone on board was assigned duties. Captain Oliver and Wayne were given two additional crew members to keep the engine and support facilities working and adequately serviced. Andrew and Stephen were assigned to their staff. These two have been part of the Tito I's original crew and had long since been in a relationship. They are the first open relationship of the Marquis Cartel.

DAVID'S PLAN

The phone in Jim and King's suite rang, and it was David. He said, "Let's all meet in the man cave. I have some information I like to share with you."

"We'll be right there."

When they were all together, David announced that their financial status is too good. The earnings from their Caribbean operation have been flowing flawlessly, and all the accounts he set up to handle the overflow have maxed out.

"We need to spend some money right away, or I need to be on the next helicopter out to establish more accounts."

The three of them looked at each other across the table. Jim summoned Keith, the Chief Steward, to bring him and King a scotch and soda and David a cola. After a few moments, David brought up the idea of King sending some of their cartel members from the

Caribbean to the "Kingdom of Tonga" to case out any opportunities for businesses that they could establish immediately. By doing so, we can upfront all of the expense money, which could be excessive, and hopefully spend another large amount buying something in Tonga long before we get there.

King replied, "What an outstanding idea David, I will initiate the phone call immediately." King turned to Jim and said, "How much should we spend?"

"As much as we can without being too obvious."

Immediately, King summoned Simon to the man-cave and told him to check with GYS Security to see if there were any cartel operations in the Kingdom of Tonga or any south Polynesian islands Tahiti in Bora Bora. In the meantime, King put a call into Marquis Island, and Aaron answered the phone.

King immediately said, "Call me back on one of our scrambled lines; I need to talk to you about something."

King got an immediate return call. He explained to Aaron that they wanted to set up an operation in the Kingdom of Tonga. And he wanted Aaron and Bryan to select 10 of their best to send them to the islands to scout out potential business opportunities.

"We need to offload some money right away."

He authorized Aaron and Brian to advance the group $2 million in travel and expense money from their Marquis Cartel rental accounts.

"Keep David updated, via secure communication, on who, when and what is going on. If additional funds are needed, ask David. If there are any hard decisions required, please contact Jim or me directly."

Shortly after that conversation ended, Simon appeared at the man cave door with the news from GYS. He told King and Jim that there were no major cartel operations in the Polynesian islands. There were local gangs, but nothing compared to Australia and Queensland, where cartel operations do exist. Those cartel operations are localized and not affiliated with the Mexican cartel or Asian cartel. With that good news, Jim told Simon that Wayne had moved out of his accommodation by the engine room, and if he would like to move into it, it's available. Simons replied that he would move immediately and thanked Jim for the accommodation. One must remember that Simon is in charge of security for the yacht. During the last month or so has been on a security sabbatical, one would say. He was still on payroll for $250,000 a year and was now put on notice to prepare their yacht security for the Polynesian islands.

KING'S TOUCH

"*That's* enough work for today," King said. "Looks like when we get to Tonga, we're going to be busy. I guess you're right, Jim let's have a leisurely trip now. How about a trip to our suite?"

Once inside, King retreated to the shower. When he walked out of the shower, he was clad only in a white towel wrapped around his beautiful chocolate body. Jim was sitting in one of the lounge chairs facing him, and his eyes were glued on his beautiful image. Despite King's small frame, he looked like "a champion of Capula."

As King approached Jim, he dropped the towel to the floor, revealing the total of his masculinity and manhood that very few people have ever seen or have been invited to enjoy. King's eyes focused on Jim's, and they begin to tear with what he said was "the deep love he had for Jim and the life they shared together." As

Jim ready himself for the shower, he walked over to the gray velvet sofa and where King had laid down. King had his hands behind his head and one leg up over the back of the sofa, revealing his total nakedness and manhood for Jim to enjoy.

When Jim emerged from the shower, he walked past the sofa, grabbed King's arm, and with just a towel over his shoulder, led both of them to the bed that dominated the suite's bedroom. Once there, King took Jim in his arms with such passion. He feverishly ran his lips over Jim's entire body, making love to every nook and cranny. King then enveloped Jim with his own body for an extended period of time until they both reached multiple orgasms. Jim and King held each other with such passion that neither could describe it because it was indescribable. The Jamaican Cartel Kingpin softness can only be measured by the depth in which he expresses his love for Jim. They both fell asleep intertwined emotionally, mentally, and physically as they plan to do for the remainder of their lives together.

King's touch was far-reaching from the bedroom. 10 members of his Jamaican Cartel have now been dispatched to Tonga to search for business opportunities. Despite his softness, his brutal and cartel ways, which Jim also shares, are well known and feared. Jim told

King that it was about time they put their cartel energy back to work.

Jim said, "I think I'll feel a lot better if I can focus on business and our relationship instead of just laying around in our silk robes in our polo slippers drinking mimosas all day."

They both agreed; it's time to get on the move again.

MARQUESAS ISLAND
"The Island of Man"

*O*n the 15th day of the voyage, they pulled into Taiohae, the capital city located on one of the northernmost islands of Nuku Kiva. The population on this island is approximately 7000 people and had the best mooring in all of the islands. Captain Oliver decided to moor at this island for an extended time while the Tito V got refitted and fueled for its cruise around the 14 remaining islands surrounding them.

Captain Oliver's plan was to stay in "The Island of Man" until the end of March, then sail on to Tonga to avoid the hurricane season. During the same time, Simon's plan was to conduct security training for all yacht personnel in preparation for their next voyage.

There were now 13 people on board "the ghost ship" as it made its way through the South Pacific. Chef Jeffrey's culinary talents were outstanding. He was assisted by Timothy, who was the original chef on the Tito I. Meals were an important part of all the staff's daily routine on board. It was a perfect time for everyone to share their experience, strength, and hope for each adventure undertaken on the water and in the bedroom.

Morale was one of the most important factors that King and Jim monitor at all times. They knew that a happy crew (gang) made for a successful mission, no matter its mission. One of the surprising relationships, since Simon moved into his private quarters, was that of he and Butch. Simon had a 6'4" frame surrounded by all muscles. Butch was from Jamaica and was of Creel dissent. He stood 5'10" and was as soft as a southern belle. Despite the fact his features were small, his manhood was totally Jamaican. Their first night together, Simon was overwhelmed by Butch's profound passion in bed. He seduced Simon to the point of submission and at that point dominated him until Simon fully surrendered. They both climaxed like a geyser at Yellowstone Park.

As nightfall enveloped the "ghost ship," all on board retreated to various locations of the 250' floating five-star hotel. Some thought of the past, others thought of the here and now, others thought of the future. All of the crew and staff feared King, the notorious cutthroat leader of the Jamaican Cartel. They also knew that Jim, who stood at the right-hand side of King, had the personality, looks and communication skills along with the polished mercenary skills that King had taught him. Together they are a force to be reckoned with.

The staff and crew knew little about David other than he had been at Jim's side for years. They had no knowledge of the cartel's wealth, which David managed through numerous accounts in various countries around the world. Nor did they know that on board the Tito V, King had hidden billions of dollars to finance their transit-specific voyage to the South Pacific or anywhere the "ghost ship" chose to travel.

When the Tito V pulled out of the harbor in Taiohae, heading for the Island of Elao, King received a secure phone call from his lieutenants on Marquis Island. Aaron informed him that he and Bryan had dispatched 10 of their Jamaican Cartel members to the Kingdom of Tonga. They would be flying into the airport on the island of Tongatapu, where its capital of Nuku'alofa is located. Their exact date and arrival time is to be determined, and a wire will be sent immediately upon arrival. Funds have been provided with instructions to locate business opportunities.

During their fourth week cruising the Marquesas Islands, King received a phone call from Dakota, the leader Aaron and Bryan had dispatched to Tonga. They had located a vacant warehouse that used to be a fish canning facility with a 175' pier that is available for lease. All land in Tonga is owned by the King but can be leased upon his approval. Dakota suggested that someone fly there immediately to negotiate the lease and secure the property.

JIM TO TONGA

When Jim arrived in the capital city of Nuku'alofa, he checked into the Hotel Nomuka. Dakota and his team were lodged in various small hotels to blend in with the 100,000 people living there. Simon, through GYS security, made provisions for them to secure all necessary firearms with full knowledge that firearms are totally illegal on all islands in the kingdom. Dakota met Jim in his hotel and escorted him to the property located at the harbor in the capital. Once inside the vacant building, which was divided into rooms, Dakota led Jim to the building's main office.

While Jim was looking out the plate glass window at the 175' pier, he felt Dakota's long Jamaican fingers encircled his chest. Soon he felt Dakota's body gently ease up on his back and when his long fingers reached his manhood, which stood as a bulge so large it could not be missed by any act of nature.

Jim turned around quickly and looked into Dakota's eyes and, without hesitation, said, "What in the fuck do you think you're doing? I'm sure you know who my lover is! Dakota, if you value your life, I suggest you put your hands in your pocket and your mind on our business and forget this ever happened. King will not only cut off your fingers and hands, but he will also ensure that there would be no trace of your very existence anywhere on this earth."

Without a word, Dakota put his hands in his pocket and walked outside on the pier. As Jim followed, Dakota said, "What you think of our find?" Such a nonchalant question after such a stupid move.

Jim replied, "We need the pier for docking the Tito V. It looks like there is shore power already prewired, and the empty warehouse can be used for a variety of different businesses that we can establish once we get here."

Jim returned to his hotel room and put a call into King on the "ghost ship". He told him about the warehouse and dock that his team had located was more than adequate. David should research the proper etiquette for leasing property in the Kingdom of Tonga. He told King that he would stay on the island until he secured the lease on the property and to please inform

Captain Oliver to chart a course immediately for the Kingdom.

Jim asked King to arrange for a helicopter to come and pick him up aboard the yacht and bring him back to Tonga as soon as possible. He needed him by his side during these negotiations. Most of all, to ensure that everyone recognizes their power. They would put David and Simon in charge until the yacht arrives in Tonga. King agreed to his request because of the desperation in Jim's voice. After King hung up the phone, he wondered what was going on, was it Jim's health? The helicopter was dispatched, and Captain Oliver was giving instructions to charter a course for Tonga.

JIM- KING- TITO V
In the Kingdom of Tonga

*U*tilizing his polished "PLC," Jim negotiated the lease on the property and permission to extend the pier to 300' from the Royal Family of Tonga. The fee for its lease was what they needed to offload the surplus money they acquired from their Caribbean operation. Within 30 days, construction had begun on the pier extension. King told Aaron and Bryan to send his group of 10 cartel members back to the Caribbean, and if he needed them in the future, he would contact them.

The first night the King arrived on the island, he could not wait to embrace Jim in his arms. They had not felt each other's energy for several weeks. That had been the longest time they had been separated since Jim's incarceration. Flat out, King cannot mentally cope without Jim's love and affection nightly. Jim without King is a lost puppy. Over the years, they had grown dependent on each other's psychic and physical dominance in and out of bed to maintain their equilibrium among the unlikely people they dealt with. One does not need to describe the extent to which they explore and execute sexual dominance to control. The world will probably not understand; they need not.

King asked Jim, "How are you feeling? Remember, you promised to get a checkup as soon as we got on a large island with medical facilities. "

Jim asked King if he could arrange for a doctor to board the yacht and have him checked out. Their surgical unit is totally set up with all medical needs, including x-ray, operating room, and the latest in hospital equipment.

"Why do you want a doctor to come to the yacht for your exam?"

"The last time I dealt with doctors in a hospital in a city, I was arrested. That's not going to happen to me again. Make sure we're dealing with the doctor that no names are required and money talks. I am very confident there's nothing serious that we're dealing with. Still, if there is, we have the medical facilities on the yacht to handle whatever may come up."

King asked David to provide a list of all medical doctors in the capital. David came back with a list of names and phone numbers for King and Jim to review. King gave Simon the list to have him run the names through GYS security just as a precaution. One doctor's name came up as "Dr. for cash," and the name was given to King. The doctor's name was Alan, a graduate with honors from St. George medical school in Grenada, West Indies. He was an American from a little town in northern Michigan called Iron River. He is 36 years old, single, slender, 6'3" light brown hair with a gracious smile (it was noted). Due to the sensitivity of this "outcall appointment," King said he would handle this interview with Alan.

King met with Alan alone in the man cave on the Tito V. During their discussion, King asked why the doctor works for cash on the island. Alan made it clear that he is a capitalist and doesn't conform to the taxation rules established within the kingdom. His belief in medicine vocation is that people have the right to explore all avenues of treatment as needed to treat their various conditions. He went on to say that he loves the men of Tonga. He has saved many of their lives, and they have reciprocated in many magical ways. He lives well and plays hard within the islands, which are his paradise. Alan said, "*black magic* does exist here."

King made an appointment with Alan to meet on the yacht the following night at 7:00 pm. Simon met Alan on the dock and escorted him to the medical unit on the bottom deck. Inside he was introduced to Jim. Alan sat down next to Jim then asked everyone to leave the room. When they were alone, the doctor started his medical debriefing of Jim. Jim explained that he and King and the crew have been on an extended holiday for over a year and have cruised over 5000 miles to reach the island of Tonga. During this holiday, he had too much idle time on his mind that he started to concentrate on his physical well-being. Aches, pains, and physical weakness that had never been there before seemed to appear unexpectedly.

His responsiveness to his lover's sexual needs has noticeably been declining. In the last 30 years, two of his lovers have been killed by war. Now he needs all the strength, mentally and physically, to ensure that his current lover, by his side, is never lost.

"Let me repeat to you, Alan," Jim said, "under no condition or circumstance under my control will I ever allow my lover to die on my watch. I have resources from all over the world to protect us, but without me, they cannot be fully activated."

Alan completed a full physical examination to include an x-ray of his vital organs. He asked to transport a portable MRI machine to the yacht to complete the analysis. Jim consulted with King, and they gave their approval. Four days later, King and Jim sat in the man cave with Dr. Alan to get his overall analysis.

Dr. Alan's first statement was, "It was a good thing you called me when you did, Jim. It appears you may have cancer in the colon. You have enlarged growths in your upper colon that need to be biopsied and removed as soon as possible. These growths can be the contributing factor to your weakness and rundown condition. What you are experiencing is not in your imagination; it is physical."

"Okay, Doc, please take care of this "pain in my ass" as soon as possible. We have the medical facilities here and a medic from the Army to act as your assistant during surgery. Check out the surgical equipment we have on your way out. If you need anything, please tell us, and we make sure you were accommodated."

"We will schedule the surgery for tomorrow night at 7 PM. I'll let you know if I need anything else."

Dr. Alan completed the surgery in less than an hour. He removed the growths and sent them to be biopsied in Brisbane, Australia, under an assumed name. He did not want to draw suspicion from anyone in the local community in Tonga. In five days, the results were obtained: **"malignant."** When Dr. Alan arrived at the man cave with the results, Jim just looked the doctor in the eye.

Jim turned to King and put his arms on his shoulders, and whispered in his ear, "We have been through tough times together, and we'll get through this one. Nothing is going to separate us."

King slapped his drink on the table and broke the Crystal glass and took Jim by the arm as they went to their suite on the bow of the yacht. Once there, they both undressed and showered to wash off the sadness of the day and to admire each other's manliness that God put forth in front of them. As gladiators before a battle, they retreated to their king-size bed in the master suite.

That morning, still wrapped in each other's arms, they vowed to fight the fight to the very end and do what needs to be done to protect and preserve the now-infamous **Marquis Cartel**.

King asked Jim, "How long should we keep information from David?"

"You tell me, King, David has been by my side since he was 21. Now that he is in his 40s, he deserves to know the truth. We will take care of it in due course; we just have to think of the right time to discuss it with him because he is so sensitive and soft, not hardened for battle like we are.

THE DECISION

*I*t was the middle of the morning. Jim and King headed to the shower to wash off their lovemaking from the night before. When they got out of the shower, they wrapped themselves in their white terry cloth robes embroidered a "K" & "J" accordingly and sat in the living area of their massive suite located in the bow of the "ghost ship." Jim put a call into David requesting his presence in their master suite, where breakfast would be served.

When David arrived, he was sporting his nautical attire for Tonga, shorts, and a T-shirt that were his usual dress for a working day on the yacht.

"David, why don't you grab a quick shower before breakfast?" said Jim as he laid out a robe with the initial "D" for him. "It has been far too long since the three of us have been together, so make it quick."

David emerged from the shower, wrapped in his luxurious terry cloth robe, and sat down next to Jim with an innocent smile on his face.

"What's going on with you guys?"

Jim replied, "We have a big decision to make, and it affects all of us. Unfortunately, time is not on my side."

"What do you mean, time is not on your side?"

The phone rang, and it was chef Jeffrey wanting their breakfast order. After the order was placed, Jim calmly and with a fatherly tone in his voice explained to David the Dr.'s findings. He described the extent to which the cancer is now spreading is all the organs in his body.

The decision now on the table is what they should do for the best of the Marquis Cartel. Stay in the kingdom and continue expanding their operation there or return to the Marquis Island, their cartel headquarters.

David seemed to take the information more calmly than King and spoke up first. "Let's return to the island. When the time comes, Jim can have the best medical attention that money can buy. We can dispatch Dakota and his team to Tonga to head up our operation there."

King replied, "The decision has been made; we're going home."

Instantly King got up off of the velvet sofa and let his robe fall to the floor. This was the very first time that David's eyes were upon the Cutthroat Jamaican Cartel leader's masculine body that Jim has so enjoyed for so many years. Now he understood why. Suddenly Jim stood up next to King and dropped his robe to the floor. David was seated in one of the chairs directly across from them both. He looked upon them as they were the gods of the Caribbean and the South Pacific. King put his arm around Jim's shoulder, walked across the room and took David by the hand, and led them both to the massive unmade bed in the suite. Once there, he unfastened David's robe, and it fell to the ground revealing the softness of his masculinity that was readied to be enjoyed.

All three of them shared the ultimate in love and kindness during a bedroom encounter, so long overdue in David's life. He had never crossed that invisible line that he and Jim had respected for over two decades. This morning was no different. King told David no matter what, he and his organization will always provide for his protection, and they will provide for him anyplace in the world. David needed to understand the "sexual bond" with a cartel leader. It is like you are bonded to King: "as your life support system for eternity." It's to be understood that many in his organization have bonded him for life.

WHIRLWIND OF ACTION

*W*hen the decision was made to return to Marquis Island, an action plan was put into effect. Jim called Jake Goldsmith and requested that he put a crew together because the Tito V needed servicing for its long voyage back to the Caribbean. Once the crew had been established, charter a plane, and fly to the Kingdom of Tonga.

King contacted Aaron and Brian, his lieutenants, to dispatch Dakota and his team back to Tonga to head up the new business venture planned throughout the South Pacific.

The crew on the ghost ship was getting anxious about the rumor that they were returning to the Caribbean Sea. Captain Oliver was summoned to the man cave to chart the fastest and most direct course to the island. He was questioning King's decision of why we were going back, and King replied only, "For now, just follow orders." King and Jim called Andrew and Stephen to the man cave as they were part of the Tito I's original crew, and both Kay and Jim felt they could be two of the most trusted onboard.

When Andrew and Stephen arrived at their office, King took over the conversation and informed them that the "ghost ship" was returning to their island in the Caribbean Sea. They were purposely being left behind to be his eyes and ears in Tonga while Dakota is heading up their new organization in the South Pacific. He said that he wanted them to supervise the construction of the living quarters in the cannery building leased from the royal family. That construction needs to be completed quickly because the Tito V is pulling out a port within the next 10 days.

Davenport's team arrived by private jet the following day. 10 well-trained mechanics covered the yacht from bow to stern going over every operating system. Yachts built by Goldsmith's company were the best built and in the world, and the mechanical team's service on the yacht was completed in five days. The **ghost ship** was ready for its trip home.

Jim, King and David summoned Captain Oliver and his sidekick Wayne, Simon, Chef Jeffrey, and Keith to the man cave for a briefing. They were all informed that the yacht was heading back to the island in the Caribbean in five days. Captain Oliver was to chart a direct course to the island. Jeffrey was to have the food pantries fully stocked, and Wayne must ensure that Tito V is fully refitted for a 4000 nautical mile journey maximum range the ghost ship could travel when fully fueled. The approximate distance back to Marquis island is 7000 nautical miles.

A few days later, Jim called a meeting on the back deck of the Tito V. All 16 of the crew and staff were nervously waiting for Jim to arrive. It was not long before Jim, King and David appeared in unison with what could be described as a "are you ready for action" look on their face.

The first thing out of Jim's mouth was, "We've been through a hell of a lot together, and the fun has just begun. We have enormous challenges ahead of us for the next couple of months that we have never faced before. How we handle these challenges will define the Marquis Cartel's existence, and none of you can deny that it exists. You have all benefited, loved, and engaged in amazing sex under the protection that we have provided you. If any of you have not enjoyed its benefits, it's your own fault. If you do not want to return to the island in the Caribbean Sea, which we call home, you may stay here in Tonga. You can become part of a new organization we are forming in the South Pacific."

Everybody was looking at everybody to see what everybody was going to do. The big question was yet to be answered: Why are we going back to the Caribbean because the security that we have enjoyed in the South Pacific is unmatched from anywhere they had traveled?

JP, one of the newest members of the Tito V, stood up and asked the question. "Why are we going back to the Caribbean?"

King replied, "We have some serious business to attend to."

The next phone call he made was to Jake, their yacht broker. He ordered a 150' yacht and two "go-boats," one 40' and one 50' to be delivered to their new warehouse in Tonga. He didn't spend much time on the phone with Jake describing the order and asked that he contact Dakota, at their headquarters in Tonga, for further details. King put a call into Dr. Alan and requesting that he join them on their trip back to the Caribbean. As Jim's personal physician, once they arrived at their island, he would be flown back to Tonga with a sizable sum of money to supplement his capitalistic goals. Alan agreed to a sum of $100,000 plus a private jet for his return trip to the Kingdom of Tonga. Jim agreed and assured him that the payment would be in cash.

Captain Oliver, with Wayne at his side, had the deckhands release the lines of the yacht, and they motored out of the harbor in the capital city of Nuku'alofa for its 7000 nautical mile voyage to the Marquis Island owned Jim, King and David just south of Miami in the crystal blue Caribbean Sea.

LAST VOYAGE HOME

*T*he first night and sea, everyone on board retreated to their private quarters to engage in a night of bliss. This included Jim and King, but this time it was different. They both agreed not to discuss Jim's cancer while they made love on the ghost ship. King and Jim have been in love so long and acted upon their love in so many places. Neither one of them wanted anything to stand in the way of the passion they felt for one another. No one knows for sure when the end will be there for either, so the last voyage together needs to be a loving one for both.

Soon they were approaching the Panama Canal once again. Simon sounded the alarm so that the crew would perform a security drill to ensure everyone was reminded of their positions, weapons and security measures for the boat. They were all reminded that the sleek black and silver "ghost ship" has traveled thus far undetected by any foe. Captain Oliver had charted a safe course home.

King called Dr. Alan into the hospital room to inquire as to Jim's current condition. Dr. Alan said that cancer has now spread to most organs in his body, and he had prescribed morphine for pain.

The doctor said, "Jim's spirits are high, and his love for you, King, is undying, and it keeps him going daily. He wants nothing else in the world than to get home and be with you where it all started. It's interesting when people are nearing their end of life; they regress back to a time when it was most comfortable and loving. Jim is on that journey home, King."

After King's discussion with Dr. Alan, he retreated to one of the small private rooms that he had established for himself in an undisclosed location in the yacht. He sat at the small French desk, with a scotch and soda in hand, looking at the vast sums of money lining the walls. On the other wall was his collection of gold and diamond-studded Glock 45's, knives, and machetes that he used so many times to execute his rivals. He would give up all of this today to save Jim's life.

On their approximately 70-day journey home, with morphine in his veins, Jim made use of every opportunity to make love with King. Even with his diminished energy, he showed no mercy in his lovemaking. Tenderness and kindness were now a thing of the past, and he also begged King to be merciless. He wanted to feel King's entire Jamaican Cartel cutthroat tactics entwine him and engage him in love while engulfed in his chocolate manly structure and manhood. King and Jim were going to make it last forever, no matter how long forever was.

They were within 10 miles of the Panama Canal. The Tito V had received permission by port authorities to make way through the canal for its passage to the Caribbean Sea's warm waters. Simon called for all hands on deck at their respective duty stations and to keep their weapons out of sight. As the "ghost ship" silently entered and went through the canal's enormous locks, everything was silent on both sides of the ship. The only conversation they heard was that of one of the lock operators commenting on the exquisite lines of the ghost ship as it passed him and motored on into the Caribbean without incident.

Once in the Caribbean Sea, Captain Oliver made a direct course for home, the Marquis Island. Upon arrival, Aaron and Bryan were standing ready to board and to welcome King, Jim, and David back home to their mansion on the island. Tied to the other side of the dock was the Tito IV, in all of its glory. It looked as bright and shiny as the day it was new. Along its side stood Captain John, who tried to conceal his enthusiasm to see Jim after this long period of time. Jim reached for his cell phone and put a call into Captain Oliver, Chef Jeffrey, and Keith the Chief Steward to get the yacht refitted, cleaned and ready for an immediate departure, at a moment's notice. He also gave Captain Oliver instructions that after the refitting was complete, the crew could take a break on the island and await further instructions.

Jim, King and David, along with Aaron and Bryan, went to the island's mansion. Once inside, King had forgotten as to the lavish lifestyle that he had established. They inquired from their island team as to their business operation in the Caribbean.

Aaron and Bryan said, "We haven't missed a payment, and the operation is outstanding; it is getting better every day. From what I understood, you were having a good time in the South Pacific, and we have a new operation underway, so what brings you back to the Caribbean?"

King replied, "Jim and I got homesick; has that never happened to you?"

With a chuckle, Aaron replied, "Nope, neither one of us has been away from home that far or that long. Do you want to send us to Tonga?" They jokingly replied.

After that, Jim and King made their way to the mansion for a much-needed rest on dry land.

THE FINAL PARTY

King told Aaron and his now apparent lover Bryan that they had done an outstanding job managing the Marquis Cartel in its incognito operation in the Caribbean. It was time for a party to celebrate. He told Aaron to invite all of the cartel members, from all of the syndicates from Panama to Jamaica to the island, and call it a "welcome home party." He asked Aaron to put a committee together, including Captain John, Captain Oliver, David, Simon, and anyone else he could think of to get it underway. Aaron said it would be taken care of right away and asked if King had any date in mind.

"As soon as possible."

Simon was put in charge of security for the party. Erin had constructed a small runway on the island's unused side to accommodate single-engine planes. Tied to the pier was the Tito IV and the Tito V, a rare sight to behold for those passing by the island. Captain Oliver had trained Wayne to monitor the yacht's radar to track any unwanted vessels or air traffic that came within 100 miles of their location. At that moment, everything was secure, and plans were underway for the grandest party that the island has ever hosted.

Jim called upon Tim, the ex-chef of the Tito IV, to contact the "Caterers to the Yachts," that they had used so many times before, to stock both yachts and mansion with the finest of food and beverage for the enormous party forthcoming.

On the Friday night before the big party on Saturday, King announced to everyone on board both yachts to come aboard the "ghost ship" for a cocktail party at 8 PM. The evening's dress was swimsuit attire and a big smile—fun to be had by all.

When King discussed the party with Jim, he said, "It has been a long time since we let our hair down. I'm wondering if t people think that we are human, or do they think we are just a figment of their imagination?"

With a little laugh, Jim said, "I guess they think all of it. They can't really know us because we can be so deadly vicious and yet so tender. The fact is they don't know who we are, nor will they ever."

King replied, "Do we want to leave this earth a mystery or a reality? We are the most powerful couple outside of the Mexican cartel that is operating in the Caribbean Sea. Everyone fears us, and everyone wants to love us or make love to us. Shit, they are so confused about who we are and what we do they probably wouldn't be able to figure it out in their lifetime."

By 9 o'clock, most everyone was on their third round of drinks. King had arranged for a DJ to provide a wide variety of music for the gangsters on board and "the caterers to the yachts" to provide food, bartenders, and waiters for the event. That way, the crew and staff could have a night off, and everyone could party without concern for their duties.

At 1 AM, the DJ and the caterers boarded their launch for the mainland. Then everyone on board paired up and, in some cases, tripled up for the night of discovery. This was the first night that David and Timothy actually made love. David had been so in love with Jim for so many years that he could not remember. Jim had protected him and guided him through a maze of discovery from the largest bank's world headquarters to the books of the world's largest cartel operating in the Caribbean. Soon David would have to make an important life choice, what is it going to be? Timothy or King? David needs to find what path into the future he will travel.

At 3 PM Saturday afternoon, the party is underway. Simon's security checkpoints had been established as before. Hundreds of cartel members from all over the Caribbean were gathered on the island rocking to several DJs' music strategically from the beach to the mansion. Food in abundance was provided onboard both yachts. As the night drew on, the group's nakedness looked like a war dance in the Congo.

Jim and King relaxed on the stern of the Tito V, gazing over their cadre of cartel members, who would rather cut off your head than suck your dick. Amazingly, these cartel lieutenants, and leaders, with no machetes, no gold plated or diamond-studded Glock 45's were having their cocks sucked all over the island. Of course, the more macho ones were bent over palm trees behind the bushes where no one could see.

On Sunday morning, King sent word to all cartel leaders to join him and Jim on board the "ghost ship" for morning brunch at 11 AM. Jim and King were both delighted to see lieutenants from their cartel partners from all over the Caribbean and the "Black Disciples" leaders from Panama. Also invited was Winston, the "Thunder Boys" leader from San Diego, who came to Jim's rescue to bring his old jail mate Jonah to justice.

At 11:15 AM, King stood up and made a toast to all of the leaders. "There is only one God among us that I have followed for over two decades through the Caribbean Sea to form the Marquis Cartel. That person is the love of my life, my partner, and the person I lived for every day. May I introduce my lover, Jim."

Without saying a word, the entire group rose to their feet, raised their glass, and bowed their heads towards Jim, and with a salute, they drank their glass empty.

Jim slowly stood up and said, "The strength of any cartel is not one of sword or pistol. It is of strength and belief in the leader they have in their leaders. Let us also recognize that without King, this vast organization would not have happened."

When King and Jim reached their master suite later that night, King asked him how he liked the party.

Jim said, "It was absolutely outstanding, and I was so happy to see Winston from the "Thunder Boys." He made San Diego an easy stop for us, didn't he?"

King replied, "I thought you would be happy; I had Aaron fly him in as a special surprise for you. Incidentally, he was quite taken back by the magnitude of our operation. He had no idea that we were so well-connected. He told Aaron that he wanted to permanently enlist his support to our operation anywhere his resources can be utilized."

"That's interesting," Jim said. "Well, let's give him a shot."

"How are you feeling after all this, Jim?"

"It's a good thing I took a lot of morphine, I managed through it. All that I'm waiting for now is for you to attack me to the point of no return in bed. Take me out of reality and put me into your bliss of love and affection that has carried me through the years one day at a time, sometimes an hour at a time."

With that, King put his arm around Jim and took him into the shower and bathed him from head to toe with warm soapy water that enveloped their bodies. When they were done, they were waterlogged with love.

Jim's internal pain was overshadowing his sexual pleasure. He slowly got up and went to the medicine cabinet to retrieve more morphine, to kill the invariable pain, yet hoping to increase the pleasure of King's touch.

Momentarily, a tingle of numb pleasure overshadowed Jim. King's Jamaican body was thrusting in and out of him with immense delight; as he heard King's moaning, the entire sensation felt unbelievably orgasmic. King kept plowing his mighty cock into Jim to achieve his final load.

Just then, Jim grabbed King around the neck, held his head in both hands and looked him in the eyes. All he could see in the depth of those beautiful brown eyes was a reflection of himself. As he watched his reflection growing dimmer and dimmer, he was crying out King's name and grabbed him harder around his neck to bring him closer for one final thrust. As King unloaded what some people would say was his final shot, Jim was numb from the volume of morphine tablets that he had consumed that afternoon and evening. He didn't feel King's quantum amount of man juice buried itself within his lifeless body.

Immediately recognizing Jim's total relaxed state, King held Jim harder and harder as Jim's body became more relaxed as he laid on top of him. King knew the feeling of death and was now accepting Jim's final breath as his final voyage home. The grand party, their movements in bed together, and their shared moments with David were now thoughts that will be remembered and shared in one's mind forever. No one could ever tell King that only three months ago, the most powerful Marquis Cartel members would be defeated by anything other than an act of war. As in Jim's story, "one must savor every day's victories, defeats, love and conquest because tomorrow it may be too late."

THE MARTINEZ MAUSOLEUM

*A*s soon as King realized that Jim had passed, he laid on top of him one last time. Jim looked as handsome as the day they met. He was always professional with that shiny personality, looks and communication skills to master all he came in contact with. He gently placed Jim's arms across his chest, took one of the black silk sheets, and covered him to his shoulders. Then he placed a call to David.

When David arrived at the master suite, King met him at the doorway. King grabbed David with both hands, with all the love and affection he could muster, said, "I am sorry, David, we have both lost our lover." He took David's hand, and they walked to the suite where Jim laid. David took off all of his clothes and crawled under the black sheet, placing his head next to Jim's with a steady stream of tears running down his cheeks, and then he blacked out from sheer exhaustion.

King called Dr. Alan and requested that the doctor prepare a death certificate and to make sure it indicates death by natural causes. As soon as all documentation is complete, we will have Jim cremated at the nearest crematorium. I will have Captain Oliver research the facilities and get back to us as soon as possible.

King got on the ship's intercom and called for a meeting on the back deck. He also called the mansion on the island and asked Aaron and Bryan to attend. Once everyone had gathered, King informed them of Jim's passing and the plans for his cremation. He went on to say that there will be a celebration of his life next Saturday, at midnight, here on the island. King instructed Aaron to arrange for transportation for any and all cartel members who wish to attend and for Chef Jeffrey and Timothy to contact the appropriate caterers to have massive amounts of food delivered to both yachts and the mansion on the island for all guests in attendance. They were to spare no expense in hosting this party.

Jim's celebration of life was on midnight, July 5. There were so many people in attendance that the island landscape was practically invisible. As King and David looked out on the crowd from the Tito V's transom, King recognized people that were not cartel and were too clean-cut to be Mafia. He called Simon and asked him to send some of his men into the crowd to identify them. Authorities from various governmental agencies, no matter the occasion, love to infiltrate gangland parties to gain insightful information. Simon assured King that if the individuals he identified were anything other than invited guests, they would not see the mainland again.

King took David's hand, and they went to the man cave. King said, "Jim's ashes are to be buried in the Martinez mausoleum as per his wishes. He wants to be buried alongside Tito, Jim's first lover. David, I cannot go into Miami for my own personal safety. Will you handle this?"

"Of course, I will, David said, it would be my honor since Jim and I have been together since I was 21. King, my life is now in your hands."

King replied, "I will always take care of you, David."

SIX MONTHS LATER

Aaron and Bryan's operation of the King's "Marquis Cartel" is over the top. They not only controlled the operation in the Caribbean Sea, but now they managed it in the "Kingdom of Tonga." Soon after King left the island with Jim, they returned Dakota to Tonga. They made him their lieutenant in charge of operations there. Little did they know that King had his two lieutenants to keep an eye on Dakota. Dakota was smart enough to know who had the real power. He cautiously made it into Addison and Jamison's bedroom to prove his worth to the cartel. The 150' yacht Tito VI and the 2 "go-boats" that Jim had ordered from Jake Goldstein in the Netherlands are now tied up at the pier and ready to go into action.

The Tito IV is still docked at Marquis Island. After King and Jim left for their South Pacific adventure, Aaron and Bryan changed how they visited the units for periodic reviews. Since building a runway on the island, they would take their small plane, flying at the lowest possible level to not be detected by radar, to visit their units. The Tito IV was used primarily for social visits and the entertainment of primary and future clients. Since the Tito IV is well-known throughout all of the local jurisdictions, they keep a visibly low profile when at sea. Aaron and Brian still call it home and roll around in the master suite every night, with more excitement than the night before.

The Ghost Ship is sometimes docked in Papeete in the French Polynesian islands, often without notice slipping into harbors at any island in the South Pacific. King and David are the masters of the "Ghost Cartel." David is still shuffling money, opening up accounts in New Caledonia, New Zealand, Cook Islands, and other countries too numerous to mention. David has used the helipad on the bow of the yacht more than anyone since the yacht was purchased.

King now gives orders without mercy, and he protects only one. David's love for King and King's love for David are both founded with deep admiration and respect. They often slumbered together as David felt secure with King's arms wrapped around him. David still feels Jim's loss, but nothing can compare to the agony he hears with King's nightly outbursts of emotion. It's so deep that *revenge* is all that he hears.

This "ghost cartel" is now forming in the South Pacific. King's lieutenants in Tonga. Addison and Jamison have continued to enjoy Dakota's manly resources. This new organization's leaders will slowly but surely challenge all those who stand in their way.

THE END

May the story continue...

ABOUT THE AUTHOR
James Marquis

*J*ames was born the son of sharecroppers and grew up in tenement housing on a farm in Iroquois County, Illinois. At the age of thirteen, he and his family moved to a small village in the same county where he graduated high school. At the age of seventeen, he moved from the small village to Champaign, Illinois, the home of the University of Illinois, and he secured a position as a teller at one of the major banks. Because of his "Personality, Looks and Communication Skills," it was not long before he was promoted to head teller. During this time frame, he was drafted into the Army to supplement the surge of troops during the Vietnamese crisis.

His distinguished military career was recognized when he received a Bronze Star Medal. His training in the Army prepared him to pursue his life's dream of acquiring financial freedom. After he was discharged from the Army, he returned to the small Illinois bank and discovered it had limited promotional opportunities to achieve his dream. James sought out and attained a position with one of the world's largest banks based in California, where he spent twenty-five years. During this time, he worked internationally in fifteen different countries around the world.

Additionally, he was recognized as the bank's top motivational speaker. After spending ten years overseas, he was invited to join the Chief Executive Officer of International Operations as his attaché; he served in that position for five years. During that time, he supervised all of the World Bank's international operation centers with the highest degree of efficiency.

Upon completing this assignment, he served for ten years as the Regional VP of Operations for Northern California. Upon retirement, he spent several months on his yacht named *The Jim Marquis* until he relocated to Key West Florida. After several years he moved to his Lake House in the upper Peninsula of Michigan and enjoyed the tranquility that only remoteness can provide. After a decade and tiring of the snowy cold winters, he moved to southern Texas for a decade. In 2019, he returned home to Sacramento, California. He chooses to reside in one of the revitalized apartments in midtown Sacramento.

During the pandemic, watching all the movies that television could provide, he wrote his first book, *1862, A Civil War Love Story*, in which he visualized Michael B. Jordan as the lead character. 1862 is the forbidden love story that involves Confederate soldiers, slaves, and a couple of rednecks from Kentucky in the waning years of the Civil War. Since its release, the book has received 5-star reviews. The writing of that book, which was influenced by the storyline of *Brokeback Mountain*, is a compelling interracial gay novel far exceeding the love between the men ever told before.

He continued to write three fiction books in a series of international intrigue, imprisonment, drugs, love lost, success and failure, and of course, love and passion. First in the series is *1968 A Vietnam War Love Story*, which is a fictional story influenced by his events before, during, and after his tour of duty in Vietnam. This book goes into the emotional side of the war. The main character takes you on a journey lasting two decades of love lost and found again, multibillion-dollar business decisions, high finance, international intrigue, and the love stories continue.

The final two in the series are *The Marquis Cartel* and *The Revenge of the Marquis Cartel*. The main characters and their lovers accidentally stumble on the resources to form a Cartel. The Marquis Cartel leaders recognize they are novices at securing the safety of the cartel members, so they enlist the support of two notorious cutthroat gangs and mercenaries. This book is filled with drugs, passion, death, international suspense, life in prison, unconditional love, and of course, a gay love story or two. These short stories have recognized Jim as an inspiring new author in Sacramento, California.